THE LAVENDER BEES OF MEUSE

Noble
Press

THE LAVENDER BEES OF MEUSE

GAIL NOBLE-SANDERSON

Noble
Press

Noble Press

Published by Noble Press, LLC
Mt. Vernon, Washington
gnoble_sanderson@comcast.net

Editing by Spellbinder Edits
Cover Art by Kathleen Noble
Cover design and typesetting by Enterline Design Services
Author photo by Travis Christians Photography

ISBN 978-0-9991386-4-9 (paperback) / ISBN 978-0-9991386-5-6 (e-book)
Library of Congress Control Number: pending

Printed in the United States of America

ALSO BY GAIL NOBLE-SANDERSON

The Lavender House in Meuse

The Passage Home to Meuse

This book is dedicated to Terry, my beloved.

TABLE OF CONTENTS

FROM THE AUTHOR

The Lavender Bees of Meuse is the third book in the Lavender Meuse Trilogy and continues the story of Marie Durant Chagall, as she forges a path of hope through the dark and difficult times of the Second World War.

When I wrote the first book, *The Lavender House in Meuse,* I had no idea there would be two more books to follow. But, as is so often true for writers, our characters have other plans and propel us forward in the telling of their stories, and for this I am amazed and grateful.

Conducting the historical research for the books has provided me with an unbelievable education regarding periods of our world's history that I never dreamed I would have reason to investigate—life in Europe, and specifically France, during World War I through World War II. Becoming so intimately acquainted with my characters, viewing history through the lens of their experiences, has given me the great gift of insight and perspective, both for the past and the future.

The observation of the peoples and the politics of many nations during the years of these world conflicts reinforced the fact that war is always an unacceptable way for countries and their leaders to deal with conflict. There are no "wars to end all wars," as evidenced by the reality that many parts of our planet are always at war, and always, it is innocent citizens that are sacrificed by the millions. Until the human heart changes, there will be wars. Despite that, in all times of conflict, there are those selfless souls that rise up to provide help and hope when needed most. Marie, Henri, Bernard, Rose, and the Sisters are examples to us all that, even in the midst of chaos and loss, we can rescue others along with ourselves through acts of selfless bravery and loving kindness.

Oh my Beloved
Would you not rise up to be with me
above the fray and discontent

Beyond the strife to a place of peace
where our love heals and makes us new

High above the fractured world
to a clime of tranquil peace
Let us rise up

CHAPTER 1

REFLECTIONS – JANUARY 1939

Rather than returning to Lavender House at the end of my long days at la Clinique Meuse, I had begun sleeping at the convent in a small room off the chapel. As my rural nursing practice continued to grow, the time spent traveling back and forth to my home along the River Meuse seemed better spent on the care of my patients. Across the many years of our collaborations, the Sisters of the convent welcomed me almost as one of their own. They had become dear friends, and I was grateful for their company during these tenuous times.

This morning found me at the convent's kitchen table, reading the Paris and Reims newspapers that my close friend Henri passed on to me. The front pages were spread across the convent's kitchen table like dark omens of doom. I read through them with reluctant diligence, gleaning all I could regarding Hitler and Mussolini's acts of aggression, both militarily through Europe and against their own people. I read the papers as much for what was not written as well as what was. The news was not good.

Last spring, with Mussolini's support, Germany had invaded Austria. By fall, the two countries had formed the Rome-Berlin Axis. Knowing war was a definite possibility, desperate attempts were made by Great Britain and our own country to appease Hitler and tamp down the march toward conflict. In September, our two countries met with Hitler and acceded to Germany's demand to claim sovereignty over part of Czechoslovakia. In exchange, Germany agreed not to lay claim to the remainder of that country. It was but was a short-lived panacea.

I gathered up the papers to clear a space for my breakfast. As if the unsettling news of the day wasn't stressful enough, the blaze of fire in the kitchen stove had created a simmering hothouse more stifling than the summer temps of August.

"Sister Jeanne, must you keep this kitchen hotter than Hades? I am suffocating!"

"It is beyond freezing outside, Marie. You need to be good and warm before you walk to *la clinique*. If you would put your coat and boots on while you are eating, you would be even warmer when you arrived."

Ah, how could I rebuff the honest intentions of good-hearted Sister Jeanne? The kitchen was her domain, and if I wanted my daily breakfast, I would have to eat it without comment. I would also eat it without benefit of coat and boots.

"*Merci*, Sister. I apologize. I do appreciate your worrying over me, and I assure you that, because of your warm regards for my comfort, I always remain well insulated long after I arrive at the clinic door."

This winter was proving cold indeed, but I relished my early morning walks, fresh fallen snow mounding round my boots, each step accompanied by dawn's approaching light. The walk made for a meditative time before I began each workday. The holidays just past were also cause for reflection. Christmas Eve had been spent at the convent with the Sisters, and my unacknowledged, muted version of Hanukkah was celebrated at Lavender House—a dinner with Henri, Félix, Bernard, and Rose. Attempting some degree of feigned festivity, the gatherings were tinged with apprehension and worry.

On November ninth, German Nazis had burned synagogues throughout Germany and Vienna, Austria. Jewish businesses were looted and destroyed, homes were ravaged, men beaten, families ripped apart, and scores sent away to camps. Hitler's expansion of hate and aggression had begun. We were all tiptoeing through our days now, our steps littered with the sharp shards of the reality of Kristallnacht, as that night was now known by. Such brazenness portended a heightened agenda of Jewish persecution across Europe.

Today was my last day of clinic for the week, and I looked forward to taking a rare three days to be alone at my Lavender House. I was seldom without company; either patients, my beloved Sisters, or friends, including Henri, were always with me. Being at heart a solitary soul, I coveted precious time alone in my treasured home.

I finished clinic at three o'clock and hastily climbed upon my wagon's high seat. Horse and I were on our way and home before dark. Keeping my woolen gloves, hat, and coat on, I settled Horse in his shed behind the house and then quickly filled both the kitchen and parlor stoves with wood from the tall stack on the back stoop. I enjoyed performing such chores, comforting rituals really, anticipating the warmth that would soon permeate my home. As I lit candles round the rooms, I thought of my sister, Solange, and imagined her doing the same. With the worries of what lay ahead of us here in Europe, my thoughts often turned to my family in New York City.

I had visited them only once, in the spring of 1923. At first overwhelmed by the constant noise and bustle of the city, evidence of growth and expansion everywhere, I wondered why Papa and Solange had immigrated to a place so chaotic. But, remembering my childhood in the busy port city of Marseille, New York City was much the same, a place that my ocean-loving father would find familiar. Where had those fifteen years gone since I last basked in the presence of those I loved? Papa had known when they left that another war was inevitable, and because I absolutely would not think of leaving France, he told me that the house among the vast lavender fields in Meuse was mine from my *maman*, and that became my refuge.

As memories fell upon me, I found myself standing before the still-resplendent mirror adorning my parlor wall, Henri's gift to me on another cold January day, in 1923. As I had done only occasionally across these last sixteen years, and rarely for more than a few seconds, I now lingered before the glass, taking measure of myself in its reflection. Having met the forty-second year of my life this past October, I knew much had changed within me but found little altered about my physical person, other than sprinkles of gray in my dark blonde hair. When I stepped closer, I saw the thin lines of age traveling across my forehead and round my blue-green eyes. Sighing, I admitted that I was more tired than I had been in 1923, at twenty-seven.

The years since had been busy and fulfilling. I had successfully opened and managed my Clinique Meuse, attending to patients and friends from our broad rural community. Henri and I raised his nephew Félix as our own son, and my work with the Sisters seemed to grow each year, harvesting the lavender from the nineteen hectares surrounding Lavender House to make teas, elixirs, lotions, oils, soaps, and beeswax candles from the one hundred hives in my fields. Life was always full and kept us all adequately occupied.

I did have some small twinge of regret that Papa never got to see what my life had become. Dear Papa died two years ago this last December, at the age of seventy-two, never having returned to France. When he failed to appear for dinner on Shabbat, Solange found him sitting still in his favorite chair by the window of his second-floor rooms, his head bowed and his spirit passed. She wired me the next morning, her surprise and grief reflected in every word of the short message. My return telegram acknowledged our joint heartache. I shared my sorrow at not being able to sit shiva or attend his service. I thought of him every day, our loving, formidable Papa.

Sister Agnès, the long-time, beloved prioress of our convent, passed last year as well. After suffering her first stroke in 1922, she survived several more until succumbing one final time in the bountiful summer gardens at the convent. Like Papa, she went so suddenly, yet for both, I was so thankful for their lack of suffering. Sister Évangéline assumed the role as prioress, and the Sisters went on as before, or almost as before. Sister Agnès had been a compassionate advocate for her nuns and certainly for me as well. She had become the mother I lost at birth, the woman whose counsel I sought during life's dilemmas—both great and small. Wise and practical, encouraging me to make my own choices, she supported me in my decision not to marry Henri when he so eloquently and persuasively asked me so many years ago. I had never found myself a woman in need of a lover, much less a husband—until Tanvir, in Paris.

The Sisters remained my dearest friends. In my own uniquely Jewish way, I felt as much a Sister of the convent as they were. I spent five nights a week sleeping in my very small room tucked into the side of the chapel. A room shared with storage boxes, spare alter cloths, and probably a few mice.

The years had been pleasant and busy, and I had been content. But I could feel now, round the edges of my consciousness, a confirmation that the world was once again stoking the fires of hatred antecedent to every war. War was the theatre of the absurd, a game played between powerful men who never placed their own lives at risk. Why did they ever think the loss of so many worth the price of power?

I sighed. Leaving the gaze of my mirror, my hopes for the future fading in its reflection, I placed two more pieces of wood in each of my stoves, stoking the fires to red-hot flames, seeking warmth as my soul remained cold.

CHAPTER 2

YET AGAIN – FEBRUARY 1939

Even with light from the lamps, the clinic was dim as night fell, turning the windows into dark mirrors. Today was Thursday and usually the day I returned to my home. Fridays were intended to be my time catching up on all things domestic. Saturdays, the clinic was open from ten in the morning until two in the afternoon and closed then until Monday morning at nine.

For the last two weeks, I had not been able to spare even one day at home but rather slept each night in my cozy convent room. There had been an outbreak of smallpox followed close on its heels by one of measles. Children and adults had been in and out of la Clinique Meuse continuously, seeking relief from symptoms. Those families with multiple contagious children I went to see in their homes, keeping the clinic as free from exposure as possible and leaving my highly capable medical assistant, Sister Dominique, in charge to triage and provide light care until my return. Many trips over many days, Horse pulling me and my wagon north and south to see the young and old, had worn me to the bone.

When I was not at my house, rough and dependable Bernard, both neighbor and friend, could be trusted to see to my chickens and cat, keeping any eggs he gathered for his own family or others. Small recompense for his looking after my home and animals. But he was forever grateful to me for doctoring his sheep and, while we never made mention of it, my keeping his hemorrhoids from flaring up angrily and turning him into an unbearable ogre of a person.

Body and mind exhausted, aching from toes to fingertips, I could not ignore much longer my body's need to shut down, to take myself to bed and sleep. From experience, I knew the more exhausted I became, the more difficult it was to quiet my worrisome thoughts. Sleep tonight would be negligible. Five years ago, I could work a long, arduous, twelve-hour day tending to ill patients, but while the number of patients had continued to increase over the years my stamina had not.

I tossed the last of the bloody gauze bandages into the waste bin and moved to the sink, scouring my hands and arms with hot, soapy water. The last patient of the day, an Irish farrier named Ronan, working the farms round the area, had suffered a bleeding ear when he attempted to come between a stallion and his mare of choice. I asked him what he had been thinking, why he had not separated them before shoeing the male. He said, almost seriously, that he "didn't think the stallion was in the mood to cavort with the fair maiden." I hoped his hearing would not be permanently affected by the result of his error in judging the amorous intentions of a virile horse.

It was well past seven, and although I could have easily slid up and attempted sleep on my hard, wooden examining table, I knew the Sisters would have a warm meal, hot tea, and words of comfort for my weary self. They were my medicine, the tonic of health that allowed me to provide the needed care to everyone that came to my door and me to theirs.

Although I was remaining at the clinic longer and longer with each dark day, I almost preferred being bone-weary at my desk rather than in the warm kitchen of the convent. The Sisters' large radio, a huge wooden box of a thing, stood in its sacred place in a corner of the kitchen, and the women sat close round it evening after evening, their cups of tea gone cold, listening for any news out of Paris and hoping to hear nothing to forecast the coming of another war.

They were still filled with haunting memories of the last war, of fleeing Paris for Belgium and then back to France, and finally finding refuge here in rural Verdun. Following World War I, the Catholic church gave them this small abandoned farm, which, after years of ongoing maintenance, served them quite satisfactorily as their convent home, with grounds enough for their abundant herb and vegetable gardens and an outbuilding adequate to process our lavender products and honey. They loved their quiet home and did not want to run for their lives or their faith again.

Everyone was fatigued these days. But more than just tired, we were afraid. So many of us that survived the Great War now saw and felt in our bones the renewal of hatred and aggression in the wind. The news coming out of Paris and London was as dark as these long-lingering winter days. Germany continued to encroach and posture toward conflict. Hitler maniacally commanded his army of terror, expanding the persecution of Jewish citizens and businesses with a myriad of detestable laws in Nazi-controlled countries. And what if they should invade our own France? My most urgent fear was waiting too long to make a plan to keep our son, Félix, safe.

Voicing once more my constant prayer to la Vierge Marie, I prayed for Félix's protection. The dear boy Henri and I had raised was now twenty years old and attending medical school in London. Dr. Tanvir Singh, my close friend and long-distance physician supervisor, had assisted in securing him a place in the entering class of 1940. Félix's English was adequate for his studies and conversation, and his intelligence and tenacity more than made up for any language deficits. He was doing well, and I was eternally thankful that I had squelched my selfish intentions to keep him close by in France, and had listened to both Tanvir and Henri, agreeing that Félix should attend university in England. Not wanting him to return to France during these tremulous times, we contented ourselves with his weekly letters and the occasional telephone conversation.

But with the increasing tensions in Europe, I thought more and more these days that sending Félix to Solange and family in New York, putting an ocean between the coming conflict and himself, would be a wise decision. The topic had not yet been broached with Henri, but I had been having conversations with him in my mind, strategizing with my words how I might best convince him, and then Félix, that transferring his studies to New York City was both beneficial regarding his education and certainly for his safety. I would not lose this boy, the only child I would ever claim, to the insanity of another war.

Rousing myself from sleep-deprived worry, I gathered up my person and satchel and took one final look round the clinic. Sister Dominique, trusted aide that she was, had laid out an array of patient files in readiness for tomorrow's appointments. I headed out my door, treading the short distance up the winding road and across the other side to the convent.

It was late now, eight o'clock, and as I approached, the lights through the windows shone bright. I knew the Sisters were huddled by their radio, awaiting my return. But I did not want the news of the day. I knew what it was without being told, and none of it was suitable for falling into restful sleep.

As though on watch, Sister Jeanne opened the back door into the kitchen, relieving me of my satchel. The others were silent and still. Perched in the worn wooden chairs from the kitchen table, they were pulled into a tight circle round the radio, attempting to catch every word streaming from the speaker. I removed my heavy coat and lowered myself into the only chair remaining at the table to remove my wet boots. Sister Jeanne brought me a steaming cup of tea, a thick slab of warm bread, a generous portion of cheese, and a peeled apple sliced into six shiny pieces. Knowing I must eat something, I settled deeper into the familiar chair, warming my hands as I rounded them to the hot cup.

The Sisters probably assumed my silence was as theirs—allowing me to better hear the news reports. But the volume in my mind was damped down much lower than the radio's, and I neither heard nor listened to what was said. I needed to concentrate hard to bring hand to mouth, biting off pieces of the bread and cheese and moving cup to lips to drink my tea. Three more children had passed today from the diseases that often take our young, and I had not been able to stop the fevers that engulfed and burned their small bodies. My role then transformed from nurse to consoler, holding the grieving mothers in my arms as they asked questions I could not answer.

Guilt and sorrow mingled with my fatigue as I said a quiet *bonne nuit* to the good Sisters and proceeded to my solitary room. My raw feelings threatened to overwhelm me, and during such times of extreme stress and fatigue, I returned to memories of the young men I nursed those not-so-many years ago in that brutal, bloody war, the Great War, the War to End All Wars, and wondered how we could again sacrifice so many. I fell into unsettled sleep, asking questions of my own I could not answer.

CHAPTER 3

BONNIE LASS – FEBRUARY 1939

"Marie, I'm thinking it's time you were awakened to the glories of the mornin'."

My eyes wouldn't open, and I definitely did not want to be awakened to any "glories," whatever they might be.

"Sister Jeanne, what time is it?" I asked, raising myself on one elbow with my eyes still pressed shut.

"It's the time breakfast gets cold, and Sister Dominique is already out ahead of you. Get up, my bonny lass, for the day is a bonny one as well."

Bonny lass? Did Sister Jeanne just call me a "bonny lass"?

Thinking I might still be sleeping and this was an interesting dream, I opened my eyes, looking up into her shining face. "And what is for breakfast, Sister?"

"Sausages and black pudding. Get ye goin' now, lass."

"Sister, has someone absconded with your tongue in the night and replaced it with one that speaks a very poor Irish brogue? Whatever is going on with you? And what is black pudding?"

"It never hurts to expand our palates, Marie, and for that matter, our tongues can speak with many accents, can they not?"

"But my question is why are you doing so?" I struggled from under the tangle of my thick down bed covers and placed my feet into cozy, worn slippers.

"I really have no answer, dear, other than that the day is a fine one and your tea is getting cold."

With that, she left, humming a merry tune, and I assembled myself for the day. My head was still too sleep-fogged to wonder further at her strange behavior. Completing my simple toilette of face-washing and teeth-brushing, followed by a brush swipe to my hair, which I settled into a tight chignon at the base of my neck, I dressed quickly, the aroma of sausages luring me toward the kitchen.

The kitchen, blessedly, was warm and empty. The radio was off, the Sisters most likely at morning chapel. My plate, piled with savory sausages accompanied by two eggs, fried crisp at the edges and milky yellow in the middle, was placed on the table with my chair facing the window that looked out to the wintery back gardens. My tea was only lukewarm but strong, and I ate as fast as I could, noting the time was after eight, when Sister Dominique and I usually consulted about the patients from the day before and those to come today. I did not berate myself, though, for the much-needed extra hour of sleep.

Beside my large plate, a small saucer held a slice of something round, black, and grainy. I surmised this was the "black pudding." But it certainly didn't look like any pudding in my past, and I did not give it a place in my future. I set the saucer, still holding the mysterious black food, atop the counter and rinsed my cup and plate. Donning my coat and boots, I picked up my satchel and set off for the clinic at a brisk clip.

The air was crisp, and above me shone a remnant of bright moon in a cloudless sky. Perhaps today would be one of sun and a little warmth through my windows. I felt encouraged; a new day with a somewhat rested body and renewed mind was always cause for hope. A smile crossed my lips as I pondered Sister Jeanne's curious affectations.

As I rounded the last bend to the clinic, I saw Henri standing on the landing in front of the door. Throughout the past eighteen years of our close friendship, Henri frequently appeared in my presence without forewarning, and I was not surprised to see him so early in the day, awaiting my arrival. My protector, my advocate, my tormentor, my consummate friend and partner in raising Félix, this man was the steadfast touchstone in my life. Although I knew him exceedingly well and we shared much of our lives, I also knew he kept secrets and concealed many of his actions, which I long suspected were aligned with French Resistance efforts since the first war. I also knew he loved me deeply.

"Bonjour, Henri. Are you here for medical reasons or just a friendly early-morning visit?" I said, walking past him to open the door.

Henri caught my hand on the latch. "Wait just a moment, Marie, if you will. I have something that needs your attention."

I tried to read his face, knowing immediately my optimism concerning this new day was likely to be dampened. "Of course. I assume you want to talk out here? What has happened?"

"Nothing as yet, but if your schedule for the day allows, I think it important that we find the time to talk this evening. Let us say seven o'clock, and I will have dinner prepared. Just knock and I will open the door into the house."

"Can you not at least give me some idea of what we will be discussing?"

"We need to talk about the options for Félix's immediate future, should the world once again tumble down around us. And we can't wait long to make some decisions. His safety is paramount to both of us, and I know you must be contemplating what can be done, as have I. I'll see you this evening.

"Do not worry, *ma chère*," he added, reading my expression. "We have a little time." He turned abruptly and left the stoop, walking quickly off into the lightening morning.

I stood nervously considering what he meant by us having "a little time." There was some relief, though, knowing he was as anxious regarding Félix as I was. Now this day could not pass quickly enough.

Although consumed by the needs of several patients, the morning marched by slowly. For my ten o'clock appointment, I completed a prenatal exam, assuring a young man and his small, round wife that all was well, and her pregnancy was progressing normally. Shortly thereafter, a large group arrived. Three mothers with six children in tow were piled into the back of a rickety old buckboard wagon, the driver a husband to one of the women, I assumed. They slowly emptied themselves from the wagon and entered the clinic in a trail of despair.

Varying in age from toddlers to adolescents, the children were covered with drying sores and scabs, their measles symptoms diminishing but not yet a memory. All were extremely lethargic, significantly dehydrated, and in need of adequate nourishment, with hollowed-out faces and wrists and ankles narrow and bony. After cleaning their bodies with soapy cloths and then applying lavender lotion to their pustules and scabs, I gave each family a jar of the ointment for soothing and a bag of green tea to improve strength. Reassuring them the worst was over, Sister Dominique escorted them to the convent, where they would be fed and sent home with baskets of foodstuffs. The larders of many families on small farms were lean, especially this time of year. I was more worried about the mothers than their offspring, imploring them all to drink water throughout the day, feed themselves as well as their children, and sleep whenever possible. These beleaguered women had nursed their young round the clock for many weeks, battling disease, worry, and exhaustion.

The next persons to my clinic were familiar visitors with no appointment. At least once a month, two elderly women from Verdun, lifelong companions Eugénie and Félicité, would grace the clinic with their presence. They had any number of the many non-life-threatening ailments common to the aged, but their spirits were eternally young. Rather than complain and insist I cure whatever was bothering them (as many did), they merely had me listen to their health concerns, asking thoughtful questions, hoping to prolong their active lives for as long as possible. They drove their motorcar with abandon, always stopping at the convent to buy candles and lotions before appearing at my clinic door.

"Good morning, Mesdames. Always a pleasure to see you. How might I be of service this day?" I asked, giving them both a sincere smile and, with a gesture, suggesting they take a seat.

"And a good morning to you as well, Nurse Durant. We really have nothing new for you to examine, but rather, we have brought you a gift that might be of benefit to your work."

The women looked so similar that, if one did not know they were but friends, you might assume they were twins. Both had gray hair curling round their heads as halos, deep blue eyes in long faces with longer noses, and their tall, slender frames were always impeccably dressed in the fashion of twenty years ago. The slightly taller Eugénie usually did the talking, while Félicité would enthusiastically nod or shake her head, reinforcing whatever was being shared verbally by her companion. Now, as one, their white-gloved hands dove into their handbags and lifted out glass jars filled with stuffings of green and brown.

"Voilà! We had an overabundance of garden herbs and flowers this year, which we have dried and crushed for you. Here we have mint, chamomile, ginger, and oregano. We find they are especially beneficial for aiding in proper digestion, both worrisome concerns for we older women. Of course you are aware of the healing benefits of these plants, and we are so pleased to help supplement your supply."

"You are correct in all respects, ladies, and I gratefully accept your thoughtful contributions." I took the four full jars and placed them in a row atop Sister Dominique's desk, taking care not to catch the Sister's eye and risk giving myself away with a grin. Turning back to my excited visitors, I waited for them to reveal what I knew remained on their minds, the true intent of their visit. They pulled off their gloves, laid them across their laps, and leaned forward ever so slightly in their chairs.

"And Nurse . . . we are wondering how that handsome Indian physician we have seen here several times in the past was doing. None of us has seen him with you in Verdun or here in the clinic for some time now. Is he still acting as your physician supervisor?"

"Yes, Dr. Singh is well and is still my acting supervisor. We communicate by mail and telephone, and hopefully, in the near future, we will meet to confer in person. May I ask why your interest in Dr. Singh?"

The friends looked at one another, raised their gray eyebrows simultaneously, and looked back at me as though they had come to a consensus. "Actually, we were merely wondering if the gentleman was married and had a family."

"Yes, he has a wife and two sons in India, where he has a thriving medical practice. He continues to teach and lecture at hospitals in Paris and London once or twice a year, thus we are able to continue our medical collaboration. And again, I ask, why your curiosity?"

They glanced at each other and began pulling on their gloves. Taking up their bags, they rose from their chairs in unison. "We were merely inquiring that if the good doctor was available, might he consider taking over the physician practice so long abandoned in Verdun. He certainly seemed a good candidate, especially since the two of you have worked so closely these past years. But, alas, having a family in India certainly precludes any possibility that he might become our neighbor. Or allow him to be closer to you, his friend and colleague. We were just wondering, weren't we, Félicité?"

Félicité nodded as they each patted my arm, perhaps offering consolation, and then let themselves out the door.

Why in the world were people so familiar to me acting in such unfamiliar ways? Shaking my head, I looked at the patient schedule and awaited my next appointment.

I was seated at my desk when I heard the door open at two forty-five, accompanied by the heavy steps of work boots. Sister Dominique greeted the patient, took up a file, and in low voices I could not quite make out took the man's history and noted his concerns.

"Marie, there is a Monsieur Galant here to see you. He made an appointment by telephone last week, knowing he would be passing through here on his way back to Reims and wanted to be seen before he arrived back home," said Sister Dominique, holding the patient's file toward me.

"Thank you, Sister. Please tell him to take a seat, and I will be with him momentarily."

Looking through the history the man provided, he was forthright and honest, stating that he had years earlier acquired venereal disease. While the effects of the disease had remained dormant for years, he feared it had made an ominous return. He indicated he had not received any previous treatment.

Rather than seat the patient on the examination table, I had him take the chair in front of my desk.

He was of short stature, broad across the shoulders, with fine, dark brown hair and matching eyes. His head was round as a ball, and in the middle of his worried face sat a large tubular nose taking up much space. He lowered himself slowly, placing swollen hands on stiff knees to assist them into bending to the seat.

"Bonjour, Monsieur Galant. I see that you live in Reims and have chosen to stop here to seek medical counsel before returning home. I assume, since you have a diagnosis, that you are currently under a physician's care?"

"*Oui*, I was told ten years ago that I had the syphilis, but only this past year have I developed problems. I do not know if they are related to the disease or I'm just getting up in years." He lowered his head, sighed deeply, and continued, "I am well known in Reims and would prefer, as you can imagine, finding help to understand what is happening to me outside of where I live. I need to know if there are treatments and medicines."

"I am a nurse, Monsieur, and do not have the license to prescribe many medications. I can, however, examine you today, compile a report, and make recommendations that you might discuss with your physician in Reims. He would be able to dispense any specific medications regarding treatment."

"I have been staying in Verdun on business, and when I asked in town about where I might find good care, all told me to come talk with Nurse Durant. So here I am, asking your opinion."

"Then let us proceed. Tell me about these symptoms you are experiencing. When did they begin and how are they progressing?"

"Being in my forties, I realize I will have some physical problems, but there seem to be more than I would expect, even for middle age, and many have just appeared in the last few months. My knees, elbows, and hands swell and ache, but my papa and grandpapa both had the arthritis. My ears ring loudly, and I can't understand conversations in noisy places. There are days when my eyes are shot through with sharp pains, all red and achy. While Papa also suffered some of these pains, it wasn't until he was much older that he complained. I am afraid I am on my way to dying from the disease I contracted and want to know what to expect next." He again dropped his head, sighed once more, and folded into his body.

"Thank you for providing an excellent history, Monsieur Galant. Now, please go behind the screen, disrobe, and lie on the table on your back, covering yourself with the linen provided." While I waited for the sound of his climbing onto the wooden plinth, I made additional notes to his file, including my observation on viewing his bent head. His scalp was affected with evidence of significant hair loss due, most likely, to the disease.

The patient remained still and quiet as I completed my exam. I saw clear signs of tertiary, third-stage syphilis, including neuropathy in his feet beginning to affect his legs. His vital signs, other than an elevated blood pressure reading, most likely due to stress, were normal.

"Please dress, Monsieur, and then come sit once again. We will go over what I have identified and discuss your options."

Again, while waiting, I made notes of my findings and made ready to discuss the hard facts with the patient.

Having dressed, he sat once more, his dark eyes expecting the worst.

"You are correct in your suspicions, Monsieur. Indeed, your myriad of symptoms would indicate a progression of the disease of syphilis, which include loss of hearing, eye concerns, presence of arthritis, loss of feeling in your feet and legs, and persistent hair loss. My recommendation to you would be to immediately seek treatment from your doctor. I cannot speak as to what your personal physician would prescribe in the way of treatment, but I must be honest in telling you that, most likely, there is little that can be done at this point. Certainly no treatments currently available, the most common being Neosalvarsan, will reverse any of your ailments at this progressed stage of the disease. All physicians must hold their patients' information as completely confidential, and therefore, I think it most wise that you return to Reims to see your current doctor or, if you are not comfortable with that, find another in the same city. You will need a physician close by to follow the development of your disease and provide whatever treatment they deem appropriate. I am sorry my examination did not provide you with better news."

"I am not surprised, Nurse, it is what I expected. I was in the war and saw many men die years later from an afternoon of relief." Rising from his chair, he said softly, "I thank you for the information, and your kindness."

"Let me provide you with some ointments and teas that will help alleviate some of the swelling in your hands and feet, as well as help you sleep."

He watched as I gathered the potions I hoped would help. With a nod, he silently took the package from me and handed Sister a generous bundle of folded francs in payment before walking despairingly to the door and out to whatever means of transportation awaited him.

I did not walk to the window to watch him leave but proceeded to finish my notes. While I wrote, Sister Dominique, as she did after each patient, thoroughly wiped down the clinic surfaces and plinth with antiseptic and placed the used linens in a hamper. We often said little to one another between our patients but always found calm comfort in each other's presence as we pondered their concerns.

It sometimes frustrated me that I could not prescribe formal medicines. Especially so when we had no resident physician currently in Verdun with whom I could consult and refer patients as needed. And, as with this man, although I could offer herbal and homeopathic treatments that would provide a modicum of relief, there was little I could do for Monsieur Galant's dire situation. However, I did take satisfaction in knowing I could provide a thorough exam, make appropriate recommendations, and provide teas, herbs, oils, and ointments to help alleviate symptoms, all the while offering a compassionate experience for a patient who now had to make peace with a future looming toward a most painful demise. Handing the man's completed chart to Sister Dominique for filing, I did not feel like the bonny lass from the morning.

CHAPTER 4

THE LAMB – MARCH 1939

The remaining three hours of my day passed in a most typical manner, patients coming in frightened or angry at their ailments and, unlike Monsieur Galant, leaving with some degree of reassurance and relief. The hands of the clock moved slowly toward the designated time of seven, when I would meet with Henri in his home on the other side of my clinic wall. I did not expect to have much in the way of an appetite for whatever dinner he might prepare but knew he would have a nice wine to ease into what I expected would be a difficult conversation.

At precisely the appointed time, my knocks on Henri's door resulted in it being opened by Bernard, which was a surprise.

"Are you here for dinner and making a plan as well, *mon ami*?"

"*Mais oui*, Marie. We are having lamb and cognac. Rather, the meat has been cooking all day in the cognac. *Ce sera délicieux.*"

The delightfully sweet aroma of simmering lamb (a stew?) wafted toward me as I stepped into Henri's small, beautiful home. The walls' muted colors of sage and straw always soothed my senses and graced me with a serenity I willingly embraced when in this lovely abode. While I had thought I could not eat at all, my stomach told me otherwise, and I was envisioning a crusty baguette with the meal.

As we ate, we spoke of small matters, enjoying this brief lull in time to savor the succulent food and red wine. Never one to disappoint, Henri did indeed provide a fresh baguette, which I used to capture every last morsel of the rich *jus.* Remarking on the splendor of the meal, Bernard reminded me the lamb came from his farm.

Scooping more warm stew from the tureen into my bowl, I said, "I hope I'm not eating one of the lambs I fed by hand just months ago."

Bernard looked amused. "Certainly it is, why do you think it is so delicious?"

Once the empty bowls were removed to the kitchen and Henri had laid a platter of cheese before us, we became silent, knowing we must proceed to weightier matters.

Henri was obviously contemplating where, or how, to begin. I helped myself to a rather large cut of soft, pungent Camembert, sliding it onto a thin slice of bread. Halfway through my cheese, I could no longer wait to pose the question. "Henri, what have you discovered that causes you to say we have only a little time to make decisions?"

He lifted his glass slowly and took a long drink, looking from Bernard to me. "In addition to the disturbing events in Germany, I have news from my sources that before the end of summer both the United States and Great Britain will no longer accept Jewish refugees."

"Your 'sources'? That sounds ominously clandestine."

"Perhaps, but also true. The German Reich is poised to implement Hitler's manifesto of terror and will stop at nothing as it plows forward to another war. I can't but think all Jews who remain in Europe are placing themselves at risk. I would suggest that before all borders close we send Félix to America. I know you have been pondering the same, Marie. Is that not so?"

"I have thought of almost nothing else but didn't know how to bring it up, thinking you might feel my precautions unnecessary or premature. I am in complete agreement with all you say. Letters from Solange continually mention how fervently America wants to remain out of any coming conflict in which Europe becomes embroiled. We both know Germany is hoping that is true, and it serves to further embolden their regime of madmen.

"Here is what I have been concocting regarding our beloved boy. I will write a letter to Solange and Philippe, asking if they are willing to have Félix make his home with them. It would be for the purpose of continuing his education at the medical college in New York City. Dr. Singh assures me it is a prestigious medical school, and he would write a letter of recommendation, as would Félix's other professors at King's College."

Henri's eyes narrowed a little, his head tilting ever so slightly. "You have already spoken to Tanvir about this arrangement?"

I met his eyes unwaveringly. It was a relief to share all that had been burdening my heart for so long. "Before any of this discussion between you and I took place, I wanted to be sure there was a school close to my family, one Félix would find acceptable. Solange and Philippe certainly have room for one more person in their large home, and since Papa's passing, there has been a deep sadness in their family that perhaps Félix might lift. He could take Papa's suite of rooms.

I think the only opposition to such a plan would come from Félix himself. He is quite satisfied with his courses in London, his many friends, and I do not think it has crossed his mind at all that only because he is Jewish any coming conflict could put an end to his schooling, or worse. I doubt he ever much thinks of himself as Jewish at all."

"It is a sensible plan, Marie. I like it. And, as you say, while we may agree the proposal is sound and to be implemented as soon as possible, the boy of ours may be of a different mind."

I relaxed, realizing how formally we had been conversing back and forth, our words rather stilted and spoken with caution. We had both been apprehensive of where the other stood regarding Félix. "We will give him no option. We know what is best for him. And if he won't listen to reason, the benefits of living in another country with a loving family and availing himself of the finest education he could hope for, all paid for by us, might I add, then I will remind him of these truths. And then I will plead. If needed, I will get down on my knees and beg him to leave—insist that he do so."

"Well, it seems going to New York would keep him out of the war on this side, and that would be a good enough reason to go. Would be for me," Bernard said quite suddenly, the first words from him since our lamb discussion.

I was still wondering why he was here with us, discussing our Félix's future. "And what else is going on here? Why is Bernard with us?"

"Do I need a reason to join my friends for dinner? After all, I brought the meat," Bernard said, perhaps attempting to lighten the atmosphere a bit.

"I apologize, Bernard, I didn't mean to sound rude. But I know better than that." My eyes darted to each of them. "What else have you two not yet told me?"

"You have raised Félix as your own son. He calls you his 'Maman Marie,' and since the day I brought the young child to your door, he has adored you above all others."

Félix came into my life at the age of four, when he appeared at my front door hiding behind Henri. His mother had died, and his despondent father left, leaving no word of where to, and never returned. Henri assumed responsibility for his young, abandoned nephew.

I had become a mother to him, and he became to me a son and a constant source of joy. During all his years before going off to university, he also spent much time around the Sisters, and they adored him. He was fortunate to have many *grand-mères*. He and I, from time to time, discussed the strong faith of the nuns. However, I never brought up the topic of any specific religious beliefs. While he was certainly taught to pray by the good Sisters, Judaism was never discussed.

Henri continued, "It would not be farfetched that he indeed become your son, your legal son. In other words, he would become Félix Durant. That his legal papers identify him as Félix Durant, born in Belgium, descended from a good Catholic family of Durants and his mother, Marie Durant, a devout Catholic woman herself."

"And you think that a necessary precaution? To create new documents for Félix because he is a Jew? As I know we all are." He and I had never, in our eighteen years of close acquaintance, verbally acknowledged in any way our cultural origins, embracing instead a quiet acknowledgment of holidays. Until now, we never had cause to discuss it, that Henri and Félix, like myself, were Jewish.

"Félix and my family are descendants of a long line of proud and successful Jews—traveling merchants and farmers. We have always kept our faith close inside. Who we are is in our blood, of our hearts, and I have never felt the need or desire to demonstrate my beliefs or opinions before anyone."

"Ha, you sound exactly like my papa when, as a young girl, I asked him why we did not practice our faith. He forbade it, always suspicious of those who might seek to undermine anyone practicing rituals unlike their own. Only years later, after the war, did I begin to understand Papa's deep faith as well as his cause for reticence. Solange and Philippe freely keep the Sabbath and holy days. But that is life in New York.

"Although I consider myself not a religious person, in my heart I hold fast to the Sabbath as well as praying fervently, when needed, to la Vierge Marie. When I took possession of my mother's family home here in Meuse, I was seeking a place of solitude to recover from the war, and Papa, concerned about any future complications for his Jewish daughter, had my birth records and all other official documents pertaining to my identity legally changed. And I became Marie Durant rather than Marie Durant Chagall." Finally, after all these years, it was a relief to spill my long-hidden words of history.

"Yes, I know that to be your truth, Marie, and I commend your papa for his foresight. Do we have the same degree of foresight to act swiftly to protect Félix? Regardless of your birthright, you have been Marie Durant for almost twenty years. It would be most fitting for the boy to truly become your legal son, Félix Durant, and bestow upon him the same protection your papa gave you."

I was quite surprised to hear this, although nothing should surprise me regarding Henri. Yet, I was certain I had done nothing to betray my secrets. "How do you claim to already know what I told you to be my 'truth,' Henri, when we have never spoken of any of it before this evening? Papa made me promise never to tell a soul. But he is gone, and you two are truly my family and so I share this with you both."

"When I first saw you at your house, all those years ago, I knew you were a Jewess. Did you not know that when you were most irritated at life, and most often at me, fretting about this and that, you mumbled in Hebrew under your breath?"

"Ha-ha! No, I was not really in my right mind during those early days, and I am not surprised to hear it was so. Papa did the same when he was worried or frustrated."

"Which brings us to why Bernard is here. Having lost his papers in a fire two years ago, his current identification papers list him as Monsieur Bernard Schultz, his Christian family, originally from Germany, having settled in France many years ago.

"Monsieur Schultz and I," said Henri with a sly smile, "have acquaintances who, over the years, have assisted us in acquiring new legal identification papers."

"Legal papers, as in forged documents. For what purposes I can only imagine," I added under my breath.

"That is of no importance—only that such a skilled person exists. Let's call him 'the printer,' as that is his livelihood, printing advertisements, leaflets, and such. When he is called upon for unique printing purposes for individuals needing to begin a new life, forge a new identity, or replace their lost papers, I often serve as an initial contact and go-between. Bernard both delivers the requests to the printer and later retrieves the new documents, which I then pass to the owners. How many times would you say we have done so, Bernard?"

"Maybe twenty times, my friend. I am thinking there will be many more. We may need to find an additional 'printer,' no?"

Henri slowly nodded in agreement and then looked at me, expecting my questions.

I realized I was holding my breath as my mind turned over this new information. "What documents must be secured for Félix?" I finally asked.

"A birth certificate, baptismal record, and identification card. I will also secure the paperwork for immigration and begin that process. It would most likely help ensure Félix's acceptance both into school and his move to New York City if Solange and Philippe were his formal sponsors. Perhaps your friend Dr.

Singh can also move forward with inquiries regarding the medical school and begin the transfer and admission process."

I took but a moment to weigh all that must happen. "All right, gentlemen, let's proceed with our plan. I will write the letter to Solange and talk more specifically with Tanvir. Henri, you must find a time in the very near future to ask Félix to come home and speak with us. Let us pray to all the gods that our boy accepts this act of salvation.

"And Bernard . . ." I smiled, placing my hand over his own and leaning in a little. "I sincerely thank you for the lamb."

We three sat quietly for some minutes, taking in all that had been revealed during the planning. Secrets long kept and now put into trust. We were all more than what we appeared, and I wondered what we might be called upon to become in the times ahead.

CHAPTER 5

LETTER TO SOLANGE – MARCH 1939

March 1939

Dearest Solange,

As always, I hope this letter finds you and your family healthy and well. Today I will not bother with idle chatter and gossip but get right to the purpose of my missive. Knowing you are, of course, acutely aware of all the world's situation, I do not need to tell you that the times here are beginning to feel tinged with fear. Once again, we feel the stirrings of war rising ever closer to our borders. How thankful I am that you and yours are all safe in America. Because of that safety, I am reaching out to you, asking that you might consider allowing Félix to come live with you in New York. I know this request may come as a great surprise, but I must turn to you in hopes of keeping him safe from harm.

While he is, I feel, relatively safe at King's College in London, we all realize that what seems true at this moment can change drastically in the next. Henri, also seeing the portent of doom ahead, has expressed great concern regarding Félix's future. I could not bear it, would not survive if any harm came to this beloved boy of ours.

I feel a great sense of urgency to have the matter settled as soon as possible. We have confidential information that within the next months the United States will impose severe immigration restrictions. Together, Henri and I are hoping to persuade Félix to agree when we present him the option of continuing his education in New York City, hopefully at the New York University College of Medicine. Tanvir assures me he and Félix's other professors would make excellent references for his admittance into that school. And might I be so bold as to request, dear Solange, that you and Philippe act as Félix's formal sponsors, allowing us to list your names as such on his immigration paperwork?

I realize this is a great deal to ask of you, my sister, and while I would like to say that if you replied in the negative I would let it go at that, it would not be the truth. I am beseeching you to please take my son, whom you know to be of excellent character, my heart's very own, for the duration of whatever lies ahead. You know I am not one to beg, but let the ink on this page give testament that I am doing so with every stroke of this pen.

Your Loving Sister,
Marie

CHAPTER 6

RED CRANES FLY – MARCH 1939

Tanvir had written early in February that he would be teaching in Paris all the month of March, and would I try to get over to see him for a formal time to discuss my clinic practice (as he was still my de facto physician supervisor) and an informal time to catch up on our long friendship. His note could not have been more timely, as we needed to discuss Félix, too.

The day following my dinner with Henri and Bernard, I sent Tanvir a telegram, asking if the next weekend would work for me to take the train to Paris. He wired immediately in the affirmative and requested I send the time of my arrival and he would meet me, as was our custom, at the train station. He would arrange, as was also our custom, for our accommodations. I was eager to discuss with him in person the plans for Félix, knowing he would aid us in any way possible. I only hoped he would agree to the necessity of sending him to America. If so, Félix would be bombarded with the good intentions of loving co-conspirators, and I was feeling more confident that all would fall into place. There was truly no other viable option.

I boarded the train for Paris on the last Friday morning of a mild March day and settled into my seat beside the window in a nearly full car. I always enjoyed these few hours of respite; the rhythmic sound of the train's wheels upon the steel tracks provided a welcome barrier between myself and other passengers.

I was excited and just a little nervous anticipating time alone with Tanvir. We had a complex history and a rich relationship that spanned many years now. He had been my esteemed professor when I returned to finish my nursing program at l'Hôpital de la Pitié-Salpêtrière, in Paris, in 1923, and our friendship jettisoned to intimacy when he surprised me, presenting himself unexpectedly at my clinic door shortly after I had returned to Meuse, his beautiful heart held out to me in his hands.

We spent that weekend at Lavender House, most of it in my bed and along my river Meuse, discussing our futures. He was destined to return to India and eventually assume his place as eldest son and heir to his father's prominent medical practice. My long-term vision at that time for la Clinique Meuse was still a dream, but one I had set clearly in my sights. There was a need for the clinic to become a reality, two needs actually: one for the people requiring care they could receive nowhere else, and the other was my own need to make a worthy life for myself.

When Tanvir appeared at my clinic, knowing the physician in Verdun had retired to Nice during my six weeks of schooling in Paris, he offered to become my physician supervisor, albeit a long-distance one. And only minutes into his arrival, we both wordlessly acknowledged our mutual affection and desire for one another. It was a weekend I could never have anticipated, never imagining that I would experience such profound physical and emotional joy.

After that, we went on that way, meeting in Paris every six months for the next two years, always at the end of his teaching terms in our now-familiar adjoining hotel rooms, discussing the concerns of the clinic and our lives, as well as renewing our intimacy. We always knew those days were to be enjoyed for what they were—fleeting, impermanent, and precious—and we captured the moments as we could, loving each other fiercely.

The day the red crane arrived in the summer of 1925 (he loved making origami cranes and I treasured the many he had given me over the years), I knew it was the end of our loving relationship and the beginning of a much more long-distance friendship. Long dreading this change, there was also a sense of relief at finally getting past the anticipated goodbyes. I had never been a woman to want anything resembling a full-time, permanent relationship, and knowing Tanvir was fated to return to India, I approached his summons with a resolve to make this transition gracefully, hiding my pain, not wanting to cause him grief and guilt.

Sitting here now, in the early spring of 1939, in the warm car of the fast-moving train, entirely in my own world, I thought back to that June day in 1925, when the note written inside the large red origami crane arrived by post. I unfolded it carefully. It read,

June 1925

Dear Marie,

My heart flies to you.

And the other note, on plain white paper, was securely clipped to the cover of a medical journal. It read,

Dear Nurse Durant,

I hope our discussion of patients this last week by telephone proved helpful. I have attached to this note a recent medical journal you may find informative. I hope, as we all do, that the promising new medications to combat infection will be available for patients posthaste. In that vein, I have data on new research showing great promise and would welcome a discussion and your thoughts from a nursing perspective. Would you be of a mind to travel to la Pitié

Salpêtrière in the next week or two to examine the research and take part in a clinical discussion? I am thinking it an urgent matter of concern, as much hinges on the outcome.

Respectfully,

Dr. T. Singh

The Friday following his notes, I met with Sister Dominique to triage any scheduled patients before my return from Paris on Monday. Bernard took me to the station (I never asked Henri to take me to the train when I was going to meet Tanvir), and I set off for what I knew was to be an emotional rendezvous.

"I've booked adjoining rooms for us at an unfamiliar hotel not far from here. It is old but quaint and has lovely grounds." He was speaking rapidly and not meeting my eyes as he placed my travel bag into the back of his auto. Knowing him as I did, I realized from his nervous demeanor and somewhat disheveled person that he had unwelcome news he was dreading to share. Steeling my own stirred emotions as best I could for whatever he was to impart, I put aside any thoughts of a romantic time together and resolved to present a calm acceptance.

"It sounds wonderful, Tanvir. I'm looking forward to the quiet, and walking the lovely grounds of the hospital is always welcome. And food—I haven't eaten well in weeks, and I plan to do so heartily and several times a day."

The hotel was indeed quaint. Probably no more than twenty rooms in a park-like setting. We had not been here before, usually remaining close to the city, taking in its noisy ambience and flair. This time was to be different, with no reminders of what had been before.

The aging rooms were clean and modestly furnished with pieces of dark and heavy polished wood, well-cared-for furniture that had adequately served scores of guests over many years passed. The door between our rooms was also heavy and did not make a sound when I opened it from his to view my own. Both had narrow balconies looking out over the green lawns enclosed by low fencing of open scrollwork. The verdigris patina of the weathered bronze so suited the ambience of the back gardens. The vivid green grass was meticulously lined with beds of barely budded spring flowers and wild roses surrounding the perimeter.

A variety of large old shade trees stood at each compass point of the grounds, where they waited patiently for their buds to leaf. The owner had placed stone birdbaths, spotted now with green lichen, under the wide-branched trees. When I opened my balcony doors, I was overcome by a welcome cacophony of exuberant birdsong. The many species of returning birds splashed wildly, ruffling their luminous feathers and shaking the water from their heads. It was a lovely scene, one that helped me maintain a semblance of serene composure.

Tanvir, however, continued talking on and on, prolonging the time before he must relate his news to me. Reluctantly leaving the serenity of the balcony, I motioned for him to come sit on the divan drawn up against the end of my bed, facing the windows.

"Dr. Singh," I teased, "please come sit and calm yourself, or I will have to call a physician before you have a stroke. Whatever is to be said can be said knowing it is all well, and I support any decisions you have made." I drew him to me and began rubbing his back slowly, as I used to do with Félix when he was agitated or frightened. It was a soothing remedy for nerves and always worked with Tanvir as well.

"How difficult it is, Marie, so I will just say the words. . . . I am returning to India. While we have talked of this for two years now, I have only just made a firm decision and felt the need to speak with you at once.

"Mother is adamant that I complete my affairs here and return to the family. She is afraid she will not fulfill her long-assumed obligation to my father, to our family, if she does not press now for my return. Her sole purpose is to reunite us all. And her fear feeds on my own, that when I return I will become a captive to a world that, in memory, is small and confining—stifling in the extreme. I fear I will never again be a part of the larger world beyond India." He paused and dropped his head. Then he turned to me with black eyes so full of loss. "To imagine the reality of forfeiting the life I now live for one I hardly remember as nothing but stagnant . . . it sends great despair into my very soul.

"I understand that we are all connected to so much, to so many beyond just ourselves and that my feelings are selfish. Every family has its own destiny and is a dynasty unto itself, replete with kings, queens, princes, and princesses. Not to mention wastrels, jesters, and deceitful uncles." He smiled wistfully.

"And you, Tanvir? Are you the prodigal prince?"

"Yes, I suppose I am. And my mother, the queen, awaits none too patiently for me to return and take up my staff. To bring right again our own family dynasty. She, the honor-bound widow and formidable mother, awaits the return of her errant, duty-bound son."

"Do you know the date of your leaving?" I asked, taking his hands in my own and looking with mutual sadness into his eyes.

"I leave after this term—most likely mid-May. I wired Mother last week, but I have yet to hear from her. She does not want to appear too eager, too excited. Not after all the years of waiting I have put her through. She will punish me just a little and make me wait to hear of her happiness. Even now I know she is feverishly planning a great celebration. I can see her making a long list of the invitees: those she knows, those she thinks she knows, and those she wishes to know. She has most likely been planning this day in minute detail since the day after I left for boarding school in London. I have not been back since that time, all those years ago. No wonder we are both afraid!"

"You know, Tanvir, you might consider returning for an extended family visit. Perhaps for a month or so, to see how it might be before you commit to returning permanently?"

He laughed out loud. "Oh, it would be very naïve of me to ever return thinking I could leave again. Once I go, I will again become a subject of India and my mother. When I wrote the long-anticipated letter agreeing I would return home, I did insist on one stipulation, the only wild card I hold resolutely in my hand: that I would come home once and for all and take up my father's practice and position, but each year I would return to Paris or London to teach a class at one or the other of the schools. In speaking with the universities, both assured me of a class on their schedules. This plan ensures I remain current in my medical endeavors, continue teaching, and also allows me to travel to the places that have become home to me. And, hopefully, ensures that you and I will continue contact in some way as well.

"But my mother has an iron will that she has honed all these years. I fear she will not trust to let go of me again, even just for a single semester of teaching."

Speaking with more resolve than I felt, my heart catching in my throat, I said rather too gaily, "But what a splendid plan, Tanvir! Surely your mother will not take issue with any of it. And how wonderful that you can create such a fulfilling balance. I am most selfishly buoyed by your intentions, knowing that we will not lose touch."

Tanvir shook his head and looked away for a moment. "You do understand, Marie, that once I return to India I will no doubt marry soon thereafter. I may even meet my future wife at my homecoming celebrations. I have no doubt my mother has her eye on many choices and now will choose the one she feels best suits her ideal of the perfect daughter-in-law. I only hope she doesn't punish my absence by marrying me off to an ugly and contentious woman! But she and I will have that discussion upon my return. I must remember, I hold the cards, even knowing she is a fierce dealer and hopes to win all the rounds."

"What a strange way for you and your mother to love one another. Deals and negotiations? I cannot imagine wanting anything but the utmost good for my child."

"My mother believes she does indeed have my very best at heart. It is just that we know our own hearts so much better than we truly know another's, and mothers assume their sons' hearts to beat as their own. And perhaps in my culture it is even more so, but I do not think that is true, as all of my friends seem to have mothers, wherever they live— Europe, Asia, India—who spend much of their time begging their sons to return to the family seat of birth. Woe to the son who does not heed his mother's call."

"Well then, I am glad I am a daughter who has had the good fortune not to be beleaguered by a papa who bids me to America. I am no prodigal princess but perhaps a lady-in-waiting."

"A lady-in-waiting? And what are you waiting for, Marie?"

"I once heard a wise person say, 'There is always something waiting in the queue.' And that is how I have felt most of my life. As though I am waiting for the next surprise—a board to break, a natural disaster, the world to go awry again. I move through each day counting the passage of time with the birth of the next baby or the death of an elderly patient, the next wound that is healing, and the next small catastrophe to be made right as best I can before the world breaks apart again."

"The world will never break apart again! We have learned that war solves little. Better to live alongside each other in peace as best we all can."

"But, Tanvir, if peace is difficult between sons and mothers, blood kin who supposedly love each other, how can we possibly be naïve enough to think peace is possible for the rest of the world, whose hearts do not beat as one?"

He squeezed my hands, now resting in his own. "I have so few answers for you. I know so little of life beyond the science of medicine and instruction. I've kept my head down and avoided all the emotions that could possibly muddy my life. War has been somehow easier to manage than relationships. Perhaps that is why I treasure you as I do. You have been my sweet oasis of joy in an otherwise barren land."

I smiled at that, thinking how our relationship was a lovingly muddied one, and the best we could hope for was to remain in touch as colleagues and friends. But, sadly, never again as lovers.

"I will always cherish our time together, Tanvir. Regardless of where we are or what we do, we will always be joined."

"I have no doubt of that. We will write, and when I am teaching in Paris we will meet for dinner. Being a married man by then, that is all I can hope for."

I smiled resolutely through the tears welling in my eyes. "And our friendship is all we need. Take heart, all will be well, my friend. There is much we could worry over that we cannot control; rather, let's insulate ourselves in hope. Your love and friendship have always given me hope and much joy."

We both suddenly jumped in our seats, startled by a loud series of knocks at his door with someone announcing that food had arrived. Tanvir rose in haste and hurried to his room. I took a deep breath and exhaled long and slowly, attempting to let go of the heavy emotional cloak I felt. And I certainly hoped there was at least one bottle of wine with our dinner.

Later that summer of 1925, my dear friend Dr. Tanvir Singh returned to his homeland, married the woman of his mother's dreams, and over the next few years produced the requisite grandchildren. And he did indeed return to teach a semester's class at l'Hôpital de la Pitié-Salpêtrière or King's College London for many years.

We would meet annually in Paris for a few days, captivating each other with the tales of our lives since last we met. Even on this trip, in 1939, we would, as always, catch each other up, but this time, most importantly this time, I would ask him a great favor.

And now, seventeen years after the profound shift in our relationship, as the possibility of war was beating its rapid pulse once again, he and I would know these days as precious ones. I sensed there were so few left.

It was early afternoon as the train pulled into the station. I saw him from my window, and immediately the tears appeared as I noted the gray in his eyebrows. I had not seen his beautiful wavy black hair since he left for India. I thought how I would never see it again and must content myself with the memories of his glorious self of all those years ago. I am sure he noted the gray in my own hair for, unlike him, I did not keep its reflection of age under an elegant turban.

Exchanging sincere greetings, the familiar spicy scent of him filling me with a hollow desire, he placed my bag into his automobile and took us for an aperitif at our favorite Parisian café. Before dinner, we strolled the grounds of l'Hôpital de la Pitié-Salpêtrière. I loved the wide expanse of the lawns, so familiar. They held memories both difficult and fond but all very much a part of my own history.

This was where I trained as a Red Cross volunteer nurse at the age of seventeen; where I returned wounded from the shells that destroyed our field hospital, so close to the Battle of Verdun; where I remained after physically healing to then take up my nursing again before eventually moving to my lavender house in Meuse; and finally, where I returned for my advanced degree in 1923. So many memories and how quickly the years had flown by.

After dinner we walked with no haste to our familiar hotel. Our accommodations, adjoining rooms as always, were in the same suitable establishment we frequented over the years and were close to the hospital.

He took my hands in his and with his slow smile said, "How I have waited for this time in Paris, a time with you again. Your eyes tell me you are tired, or worried, or perhaps both. Tell me, Marie, what is happening?"

"Do you believe another war is on its way, Tanvir? The Germans are breathing down the necks of all Europeans. I am not worried for myself but for Félix."

"Félix? Is he not doing well at King's College? Is he ill? And what does your concern regarding him have to do with the probability of another bloody senseless war?"

"So you agree another war is coming. You must know also of the Germans' stance on the Jews, the horrific efforts by the Nazis to strip away their humanity."

"Be assured, I do know, and I also know you so very well. What is it that you are contemplating regarding Félix?"

Even in my worry, I could not help but smile. "The better question is, what am I 'plotting' regarding my son? I just wrote to Solange asking her if she and Philippe would consider having Félix live with them until we see what happens here. I fully anticipate they will be delighted to take him in. The other part of my plan is for Félix to transfer to the New York University College of Medicine and finish his studies there."

"And you think he will agree to leave his university, his friends and family—not to mention his home—and relocate to New York because his maman is worried? It is not that I disagree with your intent, in fact I think it wise and would do the same if he were my son. But getting your strong-minded, independent young man to agree is another issue altogether."

"Absolutely, and that is where you play your part, *mon cher ami*. Would you be willing, if Félix can be persuaded to apply to the medical school and immigrate to the U.S., to help secure letters of recommendation from his professors? And perhaps you would write a personal letter of recommendation as well and assist with the transfer of his studies? Félix has such great respect for you, both as a physician professor and as a friend. The chances of him agreeing to all this would be greatly increased if you would speak with him personally and ensure him of your support."

"Ah yes, you do need my assistance. What might I ask you for in return?" Again, I smiled as he laughed, saying, "Of course I will become a part of this well-hatched plan. You and I have seen too much to think all will remain well with the world when a madman threatens our peace."

"Merci, Tanvir. We must act soon. Henri has learned the United States and England will shortly be closing their borders to Jews requesting to immigrate. Henri will secure all new legal papers for Félix, and he will depart as my true son, a Belgian-born Christian named Félix Durant."

"We will all play our part, Marie, but we can only hope the main character will agree to his as well. I will begin the process of requesting letters for him and personally contact the school in New York regarding his admission. When do you want him to leave?"

"No later than May. That gives us six weeks or so to be as persuasive as possible. I cannot express to you my gratitude, Tanvir. Now, let us talk of other things." We lingered there, my head upon his shoulder, secure in his arms wrapped round me. I could be easily tempted to remain here, forever together in this quiet moment.

He added softly, as though our conversation continued, "If war does come, it is likely I will be called up again to serve. Despite my advanced age of forty-two years and previous service, doctors at almost any age are valuable in war time. I'm certainly too old to be climbing in and out of trenches at any battlefront, but I suspect if Britain goes to war I will serve once again in a medical capacity."

I said nothing but instead closed my eyes tightly in an attempt to stay my tears.

The remaining two nights of our rendezvous found us sleeping together entwined in his soft bed. Our chaste and loving tenderness toward one another was edged in both joy and sorrow. Splaying his still-dark hair round his beautiful face, I was filled with an endearing and dreadful longing. After he fell into sleep, I laid awake most of each night, consumed with thoughts and worrisome scenarios. Toward morning, I drifted off, my head upon his chest, his heart beating strong and steady, lulling me to a place where I believed beyond hope no harm could befall those I loved.

CHAPTER 7

THE PLAN – APRIL 1939

Henri and Félix were to arrive at the house near noontime. We would have lunch and either approach Félix regarding going to New York as we ate or directly after. My stomach was in knots, my hands busily moving up and down my apron between setting the table and preparing the food. Old habits do die hard, and moving nervous hands always told me when my anxiety was almost to bursting.

I needed to calm myself as once again I went over all I wanted to say to my boy. Henri and I would present our initial plan and reasons why it was optimal in all ways to keep Félix safe from the ravages of another war. As safe as we could possibly make him.

The knock at the door followed by the turning of the knob alerted me they had arrived. I slowly walked from the kitchen to the front door, willing my heart to calm as I met them just inside the entry and threw my arms around my child.

"Maman, one day you will squeeze the life out of me," he said, returning my tight hug as I held him long and close.

"How I have missed you. And you are taller! Really, you must quit this growing upwards or eat more so you do not look like a starving student."

"But I am the starving student. I'm always starving. Is lunch ready? What's that I smell? Have you made my favorite?"

I then greeted Henri with kisses to both cheeks, a knowing look passing between us.

"You two wash while I put the food on the table. I only hope I made enough for one so famished." I could not take my eyes from this tall, thin young man. For all the world, he reminded me of a gangly scarecrow, albeit a handsome one.

Since six in the morning, I had been in the kitchen making one of Félix's favorite meals, *blanquette de veau*, a veal stew with onions and mushrooms in a velvety white sauce. Knowing he would love the dish boosted my meager confidence. He would eat and feel, perhaps, more open to the difficult conversation we were to have. At least, that was my fervent hope.

Henri, as always, had brought a nice wine, cheese, fruit, and bread. He poured and sliced as I stirred and ladled the fragrant stew into soup plates. Félix took his place and immediately reached for his steaming portion, clearly impatient for me to serve Henri and myself. But, polite as always, he waited with a smile of homecoming on his lovely face before quickly lifting spoon to mouth.

For many minutes we watched Félix eat. The boy was totally engaged in emptying his bowl as quickly as possible and then asked for another serving. He had indeed grown. I am a tall woman, and he exceeded my height now by half a head. His mop of thick black hair was quite long and hung into his eyes, gently waving its way down toward his long neck and around his ears. His nose was patrician, like mine. Just long enough to be noticed but not so long as to be distracting. We could truly pass for biological mother and son.

As his stomach began to fill, his eating slowed, and his dark eyes moved anxiously between Henri and myself. We were not plying him as usual with a myriad of questions about school, his friends, and his summer plans but were instead quiet—just smiling at one another and waiting for him to assuage his hunger before launching our persuasion. I wished at that moment I might have a magic potion to put into his bowl that would make him agreeable to all we were to ask of him.

He set down his spoon and wiped his broad, smiling mouth. "Ah, Maman, thank you for the delicious veal. I apologize for my appetite, but surely you will take it as a compliment to your good cooking. I have missed such home-cooked dishes." Henri and I merely smiled at him, me nodding an acknowledgment as he continued.

"Well, the two of you are certainly quiet. Which makes me think this is about more than just a satisfying meal. You have something to tell me. So, which one of you is sick? Other than acting strange, you both look perfectly healthy. I am ready for whatever it is you have to say, so out with it!"

"It is so very good to see you Félix and, oui, I am gratified that you enjoyed the food. And I will feed you as much as you can consume while you are with us these three days. *And* I will cut your lovely mop of hair while you are here as well."

"Maman, please, let's get down to the business of my visit. My stomach is turning from pleasantly full to feeling rather ill with the suspense hanging so heavy in the air."

"Have you been following the news out of Germany?" Henri asked.

"Oui, Oncle Henri. Although I am always studying, we are all—friends and myself—keeping watch on the situation across all of Europe. But certainly our country and allies have things well in hand, there is no need for worry. No one in their right minds would go to war again."

Henri calmly placed his hands atop the table, folded them together, and began with a determined though quiet demeanor the political education of Félix.

"Actually, *mon garçon*, there are many indications that that is exactly what Germany is planning. They are financially in ruin and desperate for retaliation for what they believe were unfair obligations placed on them following the Great War. They are heavily indebted to other countries, including America, for reparations imposed by the treaty agreements. Unable to pay, they are ready for a leader to step forward and take back what they feel is rightfully theirs. And Adolph Hitler is more than willing to assume that mantle of leadership.

"However, his agenda far exceeds restoring a floundering economy. Many believe, including myself, that the man has the makings of a tyrannical dictator. He means to take back lands he feels were taken from the Germans, impose heavy restrictions and penalties upon certain populations of his own people, and enlist allies with a similar bent toward Fascism to further his grand scheme, including the leaders of Italy and Japan. He is beginning to coalesce support from powerful men throughout the German political establishment, constantly proselytizing those at all levels of influence to rise up and make Germany great again."

"How do you know all this, Oncle Henri? This talk is nonsense and cannot possibly be true. Wherever did you hear these rumors of impending war?"

"I know many people in many places, men who served in various capacities in the first war and have remained attuned to all that is happening in the world. Countries of Western Europe hope to avoid war at all costs. Compromises and conciliations toward Germany's demands and aggressions will most likely become part of the strategy to avoid another bloody conflict. But if Germany and their compatriots are bent on reaping carnage once again, there will be no stopping them."

I nodded in quiet agreement to all Henri related, confirming to Félix that we were in complete accord regarding our opinion of the state of the world and, in particular, the precarious position our beloved France might find itself embroiled in once again.

I laid my hand on his arm and spoke to him directly. "Your uncle and myself, we know about what we are telling you. You understand, I know you do, that my time at the battlefield of Verdun changed the course of my life and even to this day has left a great burden on my soul. Once you experience the killing fields all around you, you are forever changed. And once you are threatened with persecution, you are never quite free again."

"Oui, oui, Maman, I know of your difficult time during and after the war. I know that your fragile state of mind is what brought you here to Meuse to heal, here to us. And for that I am thankful. But you must not press on me your history steeped in fear. I have faith that minds greater than ours, wise men of honor and sound judgment, will never allow another war."

"I am thankful also, Félix, that your mind and heart are still whole and brave enough to believe that people change. But, truly, the heart of man can be evil, and the heart of this man in Germany is preparing to wreak havoc on all that do not meet his criteria for being worthy."

"What do you mean by 'his criteria for being worthy'? Worthy in what way?"

Henri took a moment before answering, seeming reluctant to express his greatest fear.

"In 1933, shortly after Hitler was sworn in as chancellor, the Reichstag decreed boycotts of Jewish-owned shops and businesses. Jews do not meet the new leadership's criteria as being pure Germans. Now, they are beginning to be rounded up and taken to work camps. Primarily Jews, but non-Jews found to be homeless, mentally deficient, alcoholic, or unemployed are being sent away as well. Any who are deemed unfit or not pure by Hitler's Nazi party." Henri leaned forward, looking deep into Félix's eyes. "Do you understand those implications, Félix?"

Félix tossed his head. "What do Jews have to do with anything? And why are we concerned? France is free and independent. Nothing will happen to our people. This is fear mongering!"

"Perhaps, and we can only hope so. But the reality of what is happening leads many to believe there is much worse to come. And if Adolph Hitler and his armies invade France and seize our country, then he can do whatever he wants with Jews. Wherever he stomps his heavy boots of invasion, a country and its people will become victim to all German laws." Henri removed his hands from the table, picked up the bottle of wine, and poured more into each of our glasses, allowing us a silence in which to reflect and compose.

"And I assume the two of you have concocted a plan which somehow involves me. Is that why I was summoned home?"

"Yes, Félix. Henri and I do indeed have a plan; a plan to keep you safe so that you may continue your education and fulfill your passion to become a physician. Is that not what you want? To continue to live life a free man, able to pursue purpose and future without the threat or reality of persecution and possible death?"

Félix put his elbows on the table and cradled his head in his hands, sighing deeply to calm himself, and remained silent. We sat still, sipping our wine and waiting. He had heard our concerns for our country and its people and now he would hear our plan.

His composure regained, Félix sat upright and said, "Alright. I have no reason to doubt that what you both believe to be true is the reality we face. But I have only two years before I finish my studies in London, and surely, the world will not fall apart before then."

"Listen, Félix. Oncle Henri and I believe the world is already beginning to fall apart in bits and pieces, and the rate at which it will fall apart and move toward chaos is moving with greater speed with every passing day. Henri also learned that beginning in July, Great Britain and the United States will no longer accept Jewish immigrants. People are fleeing, Félix. They would not do so if there was not a real cause for concern. Thousands have already left their homelands, and thousands more are doing so every day. To save their lives.

"We believe that it is imperative that you travel to New York and live with Tante Solange and Oncle Philippe, continuing your studies at the New York University College of Medicine. Dr. Singh agrees with us, and he feels great confidence that he can assure your transfer to this renowned university. Your grades are excellent, and you are held in high esteem by your professors. Once any conflict that might occur has ended or, hopefully, passed over, you can choose to complete your education in America or return to Europe. It won't be forever, *mon fils*, but it needs to be for a while. And soon.

"We could not bear to see your life compromised or lose you under any circumstances. We are determined to do everything to keep you safe. Tante Solange has already assured me that having you live with them for however long needed is something they would heartily welcome."

My long soliloquy left me emotionally drained, but I knew we had a way to go before he was convinced, and I would hold fast for as long as I had to. As would Henri. We had given the boy much to consider.

"I respect that you have my safety as a concern, but isn't it my choice, my decision if I want to flee Europe? To turn my back on a fight that might leave our country struggling to remain free seems cowardly. Why would I agree to such a plan?"

"Because we have been where you have not, Félix. Oncle Henri and I have lived firsthand with war and its destruction of all that is good. And if it is to be believed that Germany plans to somehow persecute anyone not Aryan, then we are in more danger than ever."

"But isn't that all the more reason for me to remain here, with the both of you? To protect you? Would it not be the wisest choice that I continue my schooling, and if some calamity arises, I could leave and come home and we could be together to handle whatever happens?"

Henri once more placed his hands on the table and spoke with urgency. "You might be conscripted to serve in the French military, Félix. And not in any medical capacity, as you have years to go before you are a physician. You would be fighting hand to hand with other young men your age, expecting to kill or be killed. And for what reason? France alone lost hundreds of thousands of men in the first war, and here we stand poised again, expected to once again sacrifice our youth, our future on bloody battlefields. And if you are not killed in battle but our country is occupied by Germany, then merely because you are a Jew you risk capture and death by the Nazis. You are our only child, Félix. We will not allow you to be lost to us because of a crazed man's desire for power.

"We know we have said much today. Let us all pause in the discussion. Take a walk or sleep or whatever it is you need to allow yourself to take in what we have shared. And please, Félix, we ask for your trust."

With those words, Henri rose from his chair, placed a firm hand briefly on Félix's shoulder, and then walked to the front door. Félix and I sat in silence, watching Henri cross the road with his fishing pole and bait tin to the banks of the Meuse.

"So, Maman, you say Tanvir knows of this proposed plan for me?"

"Oui, and he fully agrees and wants to meet you in Paris to discuss the details of you attending school in New York. That is, if you choose to leave."

His face perked up. "Ah, I really do have a say in this?" he asked, smiling hopefully.

"No, my son, not really." I smiled in return and ruffled his unruly waves.

CHAPTER 8

TANVIR AND FÉLIX – APRIL 1939

Spending time in Paris was always exciting. But I was not especially looking forward to this visit, knowing I would be discussing with Dr. Singh my probable move to the United States. Not a conversation I looked forward to but understood it was necessary, especially as I gave my promise to Maman Marie and Oncle Henri. I didn't know what to think of their prediction of another war coming. I just wanted to finish my studies and get on with my life.

I saw Tanvir running alongside the slowing train as it pulled into the station. He kept pace with my train car once we had seen each other through my window. Seeing his happy wave, I had to admit it would be good to see my professor, mentor, and friend. He was a part of my family and a dear friend to Maman. I got the feeling that Oncle Henri tolerated their comradery and close friendship over the years, not quite understanding the nature of it. I did not understand it either but loved him wholeheartedly.

"Ah, Félix, my boy! It is a joy to see you again!" Tanvir pulled me to him in a strong hug and then picked up my small case, talking with great enthusiasm as we walked to his car. "I am extremely hungry, and as young men are always ravenous, let our first item of business be about finding good food and drink. Does chicken satay sound appetizing?"

"Indian food always sounds appetizing, and yes, I could eat double portions."

Tanvir talked about his latest research as he maneuvered his shiny black car into the city's bustling afternoon traffic. I listened as I rolled down the window and stretched my head out as far as possible, to watch the people and take in the sounds of the city. I did not believe there was any way the Germans could invade this place. We were too strong, and our leaders were surely prepared for any threat. I was not worried.

We were seated in the small Indian restaurant where I knew he had dined many times with Maman. With each item he ordered, my mouth watered more. Our table was soon filled with plates of delicious-smelling dishes flavored with tantalizing Indian spices. And every dish tasted even better than it sounded. While we ate, he asked and I answered all his questions about my school and family.

Tanvir, having eaten his fill, stretched in his seat and quickly dove into the real reason for our meeting. "Your maman and I had a lengthy conversation some weeks ago regarding your possible move to New York City. I must immediately tell you that I agree one hundred percent with her and Henri's assessment of the situation and the need for you to secure your education in America, away from the possibility of a war you want no part of. Your plan is a sensible one."

"It is not really my plan but Maman's scheme. And she is aided and abetted by Oncle Henri. I really believe their concerns are unfounded. And I don't like the idea of running away. It seems cowardly. But, I will do as they insist, since they have given me no other option but to go along with their plan. Maman tells me you are willing to help with my transfer and admission to the medical college. I will only go if accepted into the medical school in New York, otherwise I am continuing my studies in London."

"I am happy to know continuing your education is of primary importance, as well it should be." Tanvir reached into his inside-jacket pocket and removed a long manila envelope. I saw the postage was American and was curious.

"And, after much correspondence and discussion, your admission to the New York University College of Medicine has been secured. I have your documents of transfer and attendance here. They arrived just yesterday." Tanvir removed and unfolded sheets of thick white paper from the envelope and slid them across the table to me.

I found I was both disappointed and relieved. "Already, Tanvir? What did you have to do to make this possible? I had no idea you had so much clout."

"Ha-ha, Félix. They only needed to see your transcripts, two letters of recommendation from other professors, and one from myself. Your excellent scholastic record and quality of character speaks volumes. It was not I who secured your admission but your stellar reputation as an outstanding student. I am proud of you, my boy, and this is an exceptional opportunity for you. They granted you a place in their roster of third-year students, and after completing your final two years, you can apply to their residency program. Your class schedule has been enclosed as well."

I hesitantly lifted the papers, reading them front and back, my new legal name, Félix Durant, and my future laid out in black and white before me. My eyes lingered on the schedule, prolonging the time before I met Tanvir's gaze. I found myself unexpectedly emotional, quite overcome by my family's love. Everyone had gone to great lengths to secure my future.

"Merci, Tanvir, merci beaucoup. I am sincerely grateful. I hope you know how appreciative I am."

Tanvir gave a short nod and with a wide smile said, "Of course, Félix, of course I do. And while it is your decision, in return I do expect, when the time comes, that you will give great consideration to specializing in surgery."

His next sentence caught me by surprise. Taking a piece of red origami paper from another pocket, he talked as he folded it, never once looking down. "And shortly after you board your ship for America, I will again head back to India. If war is to come, I am most certain I will be called to serve again as a military physician somewhere in the theatre of conflict. It is not an encore performance I look forward to."

"What will happen while you are absent from your practice in India?"

"I have good nurses—not as gifted as your maman but qualified nonetheless to triage and handle minor concerns. There will still be physicians in the area who will not be conscripted and others who are too old to serve. If I am called up, I will attempt to find a part-time, short-term replacement for my practice."

"Do you still work in the same clinic as your father did?"

"Yes. With help from my grandparents, my father bought the property and built the clinic shortly after he graduated medical school. During my absence, Mother kept the building rented to another physician, with the stipulation that when I returned home to set up practice, the renter would be given one month to vacate. Mother had the clinic spit shined and polished, waiting in pristine condition for me when I arrived.

"Father was a well-regarded man in our village and always dispensed sage advice along with his medical care. My mother expected me to follow suit, but I am not such a wise man nor as politically inclined as my father. He was truly a man to be admired. I loved him greatly and always assumed we would practice together some day. Sadly, he died shortly after I came to Europe to finish my education. He suffered a massive heart attack and died alone in his clinic.

"After I completed my studies, I remained in England and then took my skills into the war. After that, I still had no desire to return home but remained here to research, practice, and teach. I finally returned in 1925, having stayed away from the ghost of my father and the persistence of my mother long enough, and faced whatever the fates had in store for me. And life again in India has been reasonably satisfying. I return to Europe yearly to teach and stay in touch with friends such as you and your family." He had finished the origami crane as he finished his story, handing it to me with a sigh and a soulful smile.

"Please let me know where I can write you, Tanvir. I will send you letters from New York and then one day I can visit you in India. I do plan to return to France after my studies are finished and when all this talk of war has ended. Thank you for the crane. Maman keeps all of them you have made for her."

Placing his hand over his heart, he said with a sad smile, "And I keep all memories of your maman and our fond regard for one another tucked away safely as well. Seeing you secured in your new circumstances in New York is the last gift I can give to her before we both depart. I know you will make us all proud, my young physician-in-training. You are a great gift to us all, Félix. The greatest gift of your mother's life."

CHAPTER 9

ADIEUX – MAY 1939

The thought of leaving Europe and my family remained surreal. Was I really going to get on this ship? The enormous white vessel stood in front of me, smoke steaming from the tall stacks. I had to breathe hard and steady, preparing myself to move forward and board the ship. I still believed there was no reason for my leaving, that it was all nonsense and panic and my family would suddenly say, "Of course we are not sending you to America! You must have had a bad dream!"

But reality had set in several days ago when Oncle Henri gave me my new documents—a birth certificate, baptismal document, and identification card. He put them in a small leather pouch along with a copy of my immigration papers. At least once a day, I took them out. I wanted to rip them to pieces but steadied my hand as I traced the information on my birth certificate over and over with my index finger. The document said my name was Félix Henri Durant, born 4 March 1915, to a widow of a Belgian soldier. The grieving woman left Belgium, returning to her grandmother's abandoned family house in France, along the River Meuse. There, alone, she raised her son. Part truth, part fantasy but now my reality.

And now I was leaving. A well-worn steamer trunk and two large dark blue valises were packed full of my belongings with my name and Tante Solange's address attached to each. Some things were necessary to take with me, but many were only packed at Maman and Oncle Henri's insistence.

"The gifts for Solange and her family are in your trunk, Félix, between your shirts and pants. I made sure they were surrounded by soft clothes, so they should arrive unscathed," Maman said for the third or maybe fourth time.

"I'm sure they will be fine, and I will see they all get to the right relatives," I said, patting her hand across the aisle of the train speeding toward the port at Le Havre and my leaving. Oncle Henri was quiet, looking out the windows and occasionally running his hands through his thick graying hair. Realizing how nervous they both were, I attempted to remain calm, keeping my comments positive while my own stomach churned. I wished the train was speeding me back to my classes in London, to my school chums, and not to the other end of the world. I desperately wanted to jump out the window.

Yesterday, I had made my *adieux*, some more difficult than others. When I arrived at the convent to say goodbye, the Sisters surrounded me like mother hens, kissing my cheeks, hugging me tightly, and giving me the strangest advice ("Be sure you dry your socks inside out," and "Do not eat anything off the New York streets."). Returning their good wishes and assuring them I would follow all their instructions, I said my goodbyes as they wiped their eyes. In that moment, I realized how much I had been loved and cared for through all my years by this kind flock of women. I would indeed miss them.

I saved Hélène for last. She was a comfortable confidante and had been my friend since Maman had delivered her baby sister. She was a quiet girl, and I often felt sorry for her. She had lost her father to suicide and shortly thereafter the little baby sister. I always felt her sadness. We had attended school together, and on the weekends, we escaped to the river, skipping stones, running, fishing, and, as we grew older, sitting up against the trunks of the poplars lining the Meuse, talking about nothing much or what our futures might become.

Hélène had wanted to become a teacher and attended two years of university. Now, she spent most of her days at the convent, helping with the gardens, cleaning, and assisting some of the oldest Sisters. Most were well up in years, so a healthy young woman who seemed to care as much about their convent and their faith as they did was a very welcome addition to their lives.

I took Hélène's hand, and we walked out the kitchen door, leading to the back. The herbs and vegetables were in various stages of growing, and the Sisters' gardening efforts were in full view as we sat on the old wooden bench just outside the shed. I glanced up to see Sister Jeanne shooing all the curious eyes away from the windows, giving us a little privacy before I left.

"We will write, Félix. I overheard Henri tell Bernard that if the Germans invade, no letters will be allowed out of the country. But of course, the Germans will never get to us. Not again. I am truly confident of this."

I kept hold of Hélène's hand, nodding my head in agreement. The future was actually nothing more than a blur right now. "Yes, we can write, but you know I will be very busy with studies, and the mail across the Atlantic will be slow. I seldom wrote from London, and knowing me, I probably won't write any more often from New York."

Hélène looked away from my eyes and out across the gardens, her own filling with tears.

"But that doesn't mean I won't be thinking of you, of all of you, constantly, and, of course, missing home. If war never comes, then I will be home soon. I don't expect to be away any more than two years, just time enough to finish my degree. I can do my residencies here."

"Well, I will write you anyway, Félix, giving you all the meager news from home. I hope it is boring and nothing of interest, like Germans at our border."

I had known for quite some time that Hélène cared for me as more than just a childhood friend. She was attractive in all ways: her long blonde hair and sea-green eyes were lovely; she had a slight, trim figure and light freckles on her face that darkened by the end of summer; and she was kind and generous to everyone. She always listened attentively to all my stories from school, and we laughed often. But I had not fallen in love with her. I had never been in love and felt myself too busy with my studies to even concern myself with such things. Many pretty girls at school caused me to turn my head to get a second or third look, and I had many female friends. But I never thought beyond semester to semester, much less into a future with another person. I was thankful, especially now, that there were no ties of obligation making my leaving any more difficult than it already was. And now that time had come.

"You stay safe and well, Hélène. Let others take care of you as much as you take care of them. I know Bernard is not among your favorite people and not someone you would have chosen as a husband for your mother, but he is a good man and he cares about you. Rely on him and Henri, my maman, and yours. You will all need each other if the times get crazy."

"And you be safe, Félix," she said, quickly wiping her face dry with her apron. "You know I will miss you, that I will be praying for you every day." She looked up at me and hesitated for a moment. "And I will be here when you come home, waiting for you. Do you think I should do that?"

"I will appreciate your prayers, but don't wait for me in any way other than looking forward to seeing a friend. I am sorry, but I do not think there is anything between us to wait for. We will be thousands of miles apart, Hélène, and none of us can predict what is coming. Please live your life any way you choose. Do what makes you happy."

"I understand, Félix," she said quietly. "Although I already knew that is what you felt, I was hoping you might tell me what I wanted to hear. I understand, truly I do. And I believe I do know what it is I am called to do." She lifted her hand from mine and smiled a little. "Again, safe travels, my friend."

I nodded, stood up, and, like a fool, patted her several times on the top of her head, telling her, "You don't need to see me to the road."

I left her there, sitting on the hard bench, and walked away with feet as heavy as my heart. I waved once at the windows, knowing the Sisters were watching from the corners.

CHAPTER 10

LETTER FROM FÉLIX – JUNE 1939

5 June 1939

Dear Maman Marie and Oncle Henri,

My sincere apologies for waiting such a long time before writing. The voyage was enjoyable, and if I had not been seasick much of the first week, I would have appreciated it more. I arrived safely, and as you assured me, Aunt Solange and Uncle Philippe were waiting for me.

They are very kind, but I sometimes feel stifled by the lavishness of their home. So much furniture, so many small items of bric-a-brac that my elbows connect with and topple. I have only broken two things, one of which Uncle Philippe says can be easily repaired.

And the variety of foods they eat is amazing. I will not be skinny much longer, as Aunt Solange says she intends to fatten me up. They are always taking me places, to concerts and the theatre. They even found it necessary to buy me clothes to wear on these occasions, including a very stiff white shirt and a tie I cannot manage to fold into shape. Lilith especially seems to take great pleasure in my incompetence.

Cousin Lilith is sixteen, but she assumes she has all the rights of an adult, quite a stubborn and bossy adult. She can also be kind and funny. Aunt Solange says Lilith is very much like you at the same age, not only her personality but her height, dark blonde hair, and blue eyes. The girl is a puzzle to me and often very annoying. She constantly plies me with questions about France. She talks all through dinner, and I actually must hold up my hand to get a word in or answer a question. There is no peace at the dinner table.

Lilith tells me that France is her "true home." When I asked her how she could possibly say that when she has never been there, she scoffs at me, saying in all seriousness, "Because French blood burns through my veins." I want to roll my eyes and shake my head at such nonsense but that would only make her angry, so I just nod as though I completely understand when, truly, I understand nothing about her. She seeks any chance to make fun of my English, correcting my grammar and accent at every opportunity, and I am sure she enjoys my embarrassment. Her papa chastises her rude behavior, but I can tell he really thinks she is very entertaining. If I could take my meals in my room, I would do so. But, of course, I am not as rude as she, and you would be very proud of my good manners. Lilith would benefit from a sterner hand, I think.

And I must tell you how much I like my rooms, the ones that were Grand–père's. I have three rooms. The largest, my bedroom, has a big square bed on which Aunt Solange has piled a mass of pillows of all sizes and colors topped by a dark gray duvet filled with down. I only need one pillow so the rest I just stack on the floor and it is really too hot for a heavy cover, so I just kick it to the bottom of the bed. No one seems to come into my rooms, so I just keep it as I please. Fairly neat, Maman, but not as fussy. The room has a matching chest and chiffonier of heavy dark wood. I can tell they were Grand–père's, as they certainly have a manly look about them. There is a settee and table under the windows at the opposite end of the room, which face out the window onto the back gardens. Aunt Solange seems to spend much of her time in the gardens. Every time I look out those windows, I see her digging in the dirt and planting more of something. The gardens are very beautiful.

There is another, smaller room off the bedroom, a cozy study with a large well–used desk, a wall of shelves, and two stuffed side chairs. This furniture is also of dark wood and the chairs have padded bottoms of some fussy fabric but are very comfortable.

My favorite part of this study is the small fireplace faced with brown and tan slate and the same stone was used for the hearth. There is a wood mantle where I have placed the photographs you sent with me of our family and friends. The one of the Sisters makes me smile, as they all look so stern and somber, not like them at all.

I know winter is months away, but I am planning on stacking a large pile of wood on the hearth long before it turns cold. I look forward to spending my evenings in this office concentrating on my studies. There are also rugs and drapes and such but nothing of clutter, for which I am thankful.

My own bathroom is on the other side of the bedroom. The fixtures are a bright white and the floor is covered in very small black-and-white square tiles. Aunt Solange (or her housekeeper, most likely) keep changing the towels, always a blue or gray, almost daily. I want to tell them there is no need to change my towels as I am happy with one every week or two, but I don't want to be rude. A bathroom all to myself! My college chums would not believe it!

As you can see, I am very comfortable, and I thank Aunt Solange and Uncle Philippe continually for their hospitality. Although I never met Grand-père, I feel his presence and have told him merci and that I will take good care of his rooms. Aunt Solange says to send you her deepest love and to relay how grateful they are that I am here and sharing their home.

Now, if I can contend with Lilith's antics and contentious behavior, all will be well. I am sure when I settle into school and she is occupied with her own studies then I can focus on my classes and spend most of my time in my own quiet rooms.

With Loving Regards,
Félix

P.S. There is a small painting hung over my desk in the study, alive with colors and swirls. It is such a bright picture. When I asked Aunt Solange who painted it, she told me you are the artist, and you painted it for your papa—that he always kept it over his desk, which I will continue to do. I smile each day at the welcome reminder of you, Maman. Also, you are to expect boxes of medical supplies, knowing you will put them to good use in the coming days. And why did you stop painting?

CHAPTER 11

OCCUPIED – JUNE 1940

I t was here. It was upon us. I was selfishly grateful that we were in the countryside and still more grateful the invasion had been to the north. The Germans had stormed through the forests of the Ardennes, sixty kilometers north of Verdun, crossing there at the River Meuse, and once more I felt the anguish and fear of war. I held tightly to the hope these German aggressors would never occupy anything French for long.

All of northern France was now a place of foreign occupation. The news from Paris told us thousands of citizens were fleeing to the unoccupied south or leaving the country altogether as the Nazis set about making Paris and the north their own. Our military was in shambles, with soldiers retreating, many hiding, hoping to regroup, or captured and killed by the enemy. We had barely put up a fight. Our generals had assured the government the Maginot Line would hold. We were so unprepared.

The Nazis now had what they desired: the jewel, Paris, our city of culture, the pride of France. Surely, they would not bother with those of us living our day-to-day lives in virtual rural obscurity. We were in the countryside south of Verdun, and if they were interested in us at all, I hoped they would but venture to our doors, do what they would, and then leave us in peace. As soon as the untenable reality of occupation set in, I immediately began hiding medical supplies. Our neighbors began hoarding and preserving fresh foods, squirreling all nonperishables away from German eyes.

Before the occupation, once or twice a month Henri, Bernard, and I would meet in Henri's home beside my clinic and share a meal, catching up with one another and all that was happening in our small community, larger Verdun, and the world in general. But sitting round Henri's table two weeks into the occupation, there was no desire for food or light banter, only the exchange of words between those who had experienced one war and were now anxiously contemplating the reality of the next.

"Always overestimate your enemies. How naïve of our military to have assumed the Maginot Line would hold off the Germans! And now we are invaded and possessed. Mon Dieu!" Henri ran his thick fingers through his hair again and again, much as I was back at my nervous habit of running my hands up and down, up and down my apron front.

"But we can draw another line. A line of resistance," Henri continued. "On the eighteenth, with understandably few customers, I closed my shop and retreated to the storeroom with my radio, listening to de Gaulle as he spoke passionately from London. The man insisted that even while these Nazi bastards hold us hostage we can and must resist."

"Was he talking only to the military?" I asked.

"De Gaulle called on all those in the military that had fled to safety or had escaped to re-engage and carry on, fighting again as soldiers of France knowing that Britain would fight as well, and he insinuated that America would soon join the war. But he was essentially speaking to the soul of every individual French citizen, encouraging all of us to find ways to resist at every opportunity. To provide any assistance in every way possible."

"When I am in Verdun, Henri, the soldiers walk our streets as if they own them, as if our country has been theirs all along. And our citizens smile at them like these pariahs are on but an extended holiday, and we are to make them feel welcome. I can barely contain my anger."

"I would take pleasure in strangling every one of their ugly Nazi necks," said Bernard loudly, pounding his heavy fist upon the table. "But if we can't kill them, let's make their Nazi lives miserable."

Henri became quiet, sitting back and listening to Bernard and myself haranguing the unfairness of it all, our angry fear filling the air with bitter acrimony.

He leaned forward again, looking between us. "We have a right to our anger, but it serves us no value. Anger and fear only waste our energy and cloud our thinking. Every time we sit bemoaning our situation, they win another battle. It is important to remember that our freedom is in our response and not in our circumstances. And, oui, there are opportunities for us to resist. There are many of us who welcome the occasions when we can turn our anger into action. We have time to watch and wait. The Germans are most likely here for a long while, long enough to test our mettle. The reports from Paris are not good. The Germans are enforcing more and more restrictions upon the Jews, and their situation will continue to worsen. Bernard and I both have our new documents and should be relatively safe. Bernard is still a Schultz but can now prove his lineage to the Germanic Christian line of Schultz.

"We will continue our printing work, helping to ensure the safety of those that cannot do so for themselves." Henri was sounding more like Papa every day, seeing opportunity rather than defeat.

"And what is your name, Henri? What must I call you?"

"You call me what you always have, Marie."

The warm days of summer turned to fall and fall to a frigid winter. The food rationing program, implemented by the Germans in September, was another assault upon the citizens of France. People in Verdun lined up with their cards for small portions of meat, bread, milk, flour, sugar, coffee—all foodstuffs. We heard the queues in Paris were now blocks long, people waiting for food that was now being sent to Germany's citizens and the Nazi troops. They were using our country's bounty to further destroy us. To further humiliate us.

In Verdun, we were more fortunate than Parisians. While we, too, stood in the lines for our allotments, we had our land and the stores from our summer gardens that we hurriedly dried or canned and hid. Henri found a large stash of canning jars sealed tightly in cardboard boxes in the recesses of the dusty attic of his business offices in Verdun. He distributed them to the Sisters, Bernard and Rose, and others in the vicinity, and by the end of September, everyone picked their gardens bare, preserving anything and everything that was edible, and then planted cold crops. And we had our chickens and their eggs.

My Lavender House was the "safe food house," as the soldiers, for some obscure reason, were rumored to be fearful of the bees covering my lavender fields and had yet to set foot on my property. However, knowing that when the lavender blossoms grew dry on their stems and the bees took to their hives for the winter, the risk of the soldiers' coming grew greater. Through the fall, the standing hives were still plentiful, and bees lingered in the air, seeking the very last of the year's lavender nectar. But not in winter, and winter would be long and hard if the food dried up along with the lavender.

"When winter comes and the Germans decide it is safe to venture about my property, they will abscond with our animals, our food for winter."

"No worries, Marie," said Bernard. "We will simply move the chickens into your house. Along with the rabbits and probably a goat. We will be fine all winter."

"Chickens in my house, Bernard?"

"Oui, and four rabbits," he said, smiling brightly, a rare occurrence for him.

"My house is a home, Bernard, not a barn."

"They are both made of wood and stone, yes?"

I looked to Henri for support, but he kept his eyes down and with that grin upon his face clearly agreed with Bernard, finding my reluctance amusing. My house would smell terrible, but that surely would not deter the Germans.

"And who will clean up after all these animals?" I asked Bernard, hands planted squarely on my narrow hips.

"The same person that takes care of them now: me. But not to worry, I won't bring in pigs or sheep." He winked at Henri.

I murmured that I supposed that was some consolation and bid them both *adieu*. My thoughts, as always, turned to my Félix. He was away safe, and that was my salve and my assurance that I could risk more of myself.

CHAPTER 12

THE COMMANDANT – JULY 1940

These days, I seldom ventured into Verdun, but hoping to find much-needed thread and needles, I climbed atop my wagon and headed north. The day was deceptively warm and sunny, and I was thankful to have Horse and wagon moving me forward. They were my armaments against the attitudes of haughty entitlement I knew would meet me in town. The Nazi soldiers spewed poison into our very soil with every step of their shiny leather boots, sidearms laid confidently against their liveried uniforms as they strolled arrogantly through the streets and along our homes and businesses. The sunshine did nothing to disguise their acrid presence.

And the French populace of Verdun? Many of the young women still dressed, smiled, and walked the town as though it were merely another summer's day with the town full of welcome visitors. The city's police seemed ambivalent, quite friendly to the soldiers. But the old women and the old men walked as quickly as their aged legs allowed, a sneer of fearful contempt on their faces as they hurried back into the safe confines of their homes. And persons such as I, of an age to remember the last war, assumed a feigned, resigned forbearance. It was a ruse on our part, for while we were hostages, we certainly did not have to acquiesce our souls or let go our spirit of resistance.

Surprisingly, I did find packs of needles and several spools of colored thread as well as seven skeins of mismatched yarn and an old wooden bucket I bought, because it was worn and sturdy and reminded me of myself. I stashed the smaller items in the bucket and put it into the back of my wagon. Refusing to be intimidated by our occupiers, I decided to walk along the street to my favorite café. It was one of the older cafés of Verdun, small and quaint, with a working kitchen garden out the back off the tidy flagstone patio. Its ceiling was a wooden pergola, thick with green ivies and climbing roses cascading across the overhead trellises. That is where I would sit today, admiring the beauty and enjoying the scents of the edible flowers and herbs used every day by the cooking staff.

Drat! As I was about to enter, I found my lovely café occupied by a crowded cluster of German soldiers, their attention riveted on a single man seated outside at one of the small, round, wooden tables. Here, I assumed because of his age and the number of shiny medals on his chest, was a senior officer holding court with his young commands. The confident young men hung on his every word, their devoted faces dissolving into conspiratorial laughter at his comments. They all believed this café, our town, our country was now German and that they held the keys to our very survival. That we were all to submit if we were to survive.

I slowed my pace and finally paused to watch them. This officer, so sure of his place in our beautiful Verdun, was of medium build, not a tall man, and certainly not well disposed of face or body; a nondescript person, really. His military cap placed securely on his head did not completely contain his dark hair, beginning to gray at the temples. When he glanced my way, I was pierced by what I saw in his clear blue eyes. Hunger, determination, fear, anger, and perhaps insecurity? Or perhaps that is what I wanted to see. I held his gaze until he looked away, and I continued walking slowly past the café with an unhurried step, my heart pounding as I rounded the corner, circling back to Horse. Lunch forgotten, my mind whirled from this brief brush with our invaders. I knew full well I would be encountering again this vile person. I climbed onto my seat, snapped the reins, and Horse took off at a brisk trot toward home. I liked to think my loyal equine companion felt the same anger and frustration as I did.

A week later, late afternoon on a Saturday, I was finished with patients but, as usual, stayed to complete my notes and set the clinic supplies in order, ensuring Sister Dominique had restocked the cabinets and shelves for next week.

I heard a familiar automobile come to a sudden halt outside my door, with the certain premonition that my clinic had been found and was now to become contaminated. With great confidence, he knocked once, loudly, and the door swung open. Without waiting for an "*Entrez*," he limped boldly into my clinic and found me standing casually beside my desk. I knew by the look on his face that he remembered seeing me that day as I walked past the café.

"Bonjour, Mademoiselle. I am Kommandant Friedrich Reichenbach, the Führer's representative in Verdun and its surroundings. I am completing an assessment of all businesses and establishments and making my introductions to the townspeople."

He made no mention of our steely, silent exchange with one another, and I certainly would not bring it to his attention. I merely continued standing in my place as he slowly began walking the perimeter of the clinic.

"I am told you are the resident nurse here and provide what care a nurse can give to people coming to your door. Why do they not just see the doctor in town?"

"This clinic was established in 1923, when there was no doctor in Verdun and would not be another for many years. People are creatures of habit, and many have continued to seek care where it is familiar. I see new patients as well. And I am more than qualified to treat them and refer them to the good doctor as needed."

"And you make these decisions, Mademoiselle, when to refer to a physician? You must indeed be highly qualified. My inquiries as to your services have all met with comments of high regard. Even Herr Doktor holds you in high esteem."

I remained silent while he continued his measured pacing, his left leg stiff, not bending at the knee, and appearing slightly shorter than the right. The limp was pronounced but did not deter him in his mission to slowly and with intense focus circumnavigate my space. He touched and examined closely every object that set upon the counters of the clinic and atop Sister Dominique's and my desks.

We kept our clinic spotlessly clean. His tainted, inquiring fingers would find no dust here, but I knew that was not his intent as he continued marking what he believed to be his newfound property. He would be granted no information other than what I had imparted, neither would he find gossip or chitchat.

He turned to face me, his right eye blinking quickly, startling me with two spasmodic twitches of his eyelid. I barely caught myself before physically reacting.

"And would you be willing to see my men, Mademoiselle, should they need your services?"

"If they had maladies or injuries and could not be seen by the town physician, and I cannot imagine he would not accommodate them as patients, then I would. We turn no one away."

"And are you part of the convent of nuns across the way? This is a Catholic clinic?"

"As I said, we see everyone. The good Sisters and I provide care in many ways to those in need." I realized I had, with intention, just aligned myself to the Sisters, implying without admission that I was part of the convent. He might even think me a nun. At the very least, I hoped he assumed I was a pious Catholic nurse.

"Ah, I see. You and the good Sisters. Do they also work here in this place?"

"Oui, Sister Dominique is my assistant, and the others provide help as needed."

"How very fortunate for those living close by to have such godly women of high virtue to tend them. Do let me know if you have need of supplies or the like, Mademoiselle, as I would be willing to be of any assistance. Your country is now mine as well, and I am here to serve.

"Auf Wiedersehen . . . and I do hope you found an adequate place for lunch last week in town. I am very good at remembering faces as, I see, are you."

I had not moved a step since he entered la Clinique Meuse. It wasn't until I heard him drive off that I hastened to the door and secured the lock with cold, trembling fingers. My heart was once again pounding fast and loud in my head, bile rising in my throat. I sank into the chair nearest the door, attempting to slow my breathing and calm my spirit.

Hatred coursed through every fiber within me. I did not want to engage the enemy once again, but it wasn't to be my choice. The enemy had sought me out and I would not cower nor hide. This would be my war of another kind. In this battle, I would not be at the front, called upon to clean corpulent wounds, to dig through bleeding flesh to find bullets, or to hold a man's leg steady for a grisly amputation. This enemy would engage my wits, my cunning, and test my courage. This commandant would return and, I intuited, would find frequent reason to do so, for he enjoyed this game of interrogation and intimidation. But what had I to fear? Nothing. Félix was safe in New York with my family. I had survived one war, intact enough and wiser by far, and found myself ready to fight another.

CHAPTER 13

THE BASTARD – JULY 1940

Henri and Bernard were due within the hour. I would make them a nice savory omelet with fresh eggs filled with vegetables from my garden. And bread, Henri always found the best cheese and bread. We met now every few weeks or so in my home. When one of the three of us requested a "lunch," we gathered here for a meal to share concerns and news. Always we met around food, as it aroused little suspicion and we were incessantly hungry.

Henri knocked his usual greeting on my front door, three quick, successive knocks upon the wood, and waited for me to see them in. "Bonjour, Marie. It smells delicious," he said, sliding past me with a large baguette and a small bundle wrapped in a tea towel. Bernard followed with a silent nod hello.

"All is ready, just come sit. Thank you for bringing bread, Henri. You know I always assume you will do so. And cheese, did you bring cheese? I realize it is becoming hard to find."

"Do you even need to ask? Today, I have a beautiful Brie de Melun."

We had barely sat down and had the food on our plates before I told them about my first sighting of German Commandant Reichenbach in Verdun and his subsequent visit yesterday to la Clinique. Sharing what had occurred was a great relief but I did not expect Bernard's reaction.

"Let me just kill the bastard and be done with him!" he stormed, slamming his palm on the table.

"He will not be so hard to deal with, *mon ami*. I have seen him in his favorite café eating his requested weekly ration of borscht. He may not be all he seems . . . but perhaps more," Henri remarked calmly.

"Any day, he will show himself at the convent and scare the Sisters. Why is he bothering the women? I would love his ugly face to show up at my barn for his inspection. He would find more than he bargained for," Bernard continued.

"Calm yourself. He pesters the women because he feels he can intimidate them. That they are weak, overwhelmed, and awed by his status. Ha! They do not know our women here in Meuse. However much he provokes, I think it wise, Marie, if you and the Sisters maintain a cautious demeanor with the man. Don't arouse his ire needlessly."

"He provokes my hatred, Henri, not any semblance of fear. I, too, understand he is posturing with his power and attempting to intimidate. And I will hold my tongue and my hand but only to the degree that he does not cross civil boundaries. I see deep fear and a festering anger in his eyes. I think he is not a stable person but, in fact, greatly damaged. The Sisters and I would be fools not to have a healthy caution of him."

"Do you want me to have some of the boys take watches between the convent and clinic? They would be happy to find themselves on lookout. I know I look forward to making his acquaintance."

"That is not necessary, Bernard. I will keep you apprised if his "inspections" become too frequent and bothersome to my patients. The Sisters are always in one another's company, and I know they would not hesitate to protect each other should it become necessary, which I do not think it will. He wants something from me, but as yet, I do not know what. I do not expect the Sisters to be threatened in the same way."

A look passed between the two men. I did not want to pursue discussing the commandant any more at this point. But I would heed Henri's advice and tread lightly in his presence. And although the German was a man rightly to be feared, I would not cower in the face of his provoking demeanor. He was tortured. I could see a haunting in his eyes, the eye that twitched when he became intense. Oui, I would tread lightly.

"Do you know, ma chère, if the commandant has become aware that you have a home to the south?" Henri asked, tearing off another piece of bread and pulling the cheese closer.

"No, I think he believes me to be some sort of nursing nun and assumes I live at the convent. If he does find out about my home, which I'm sure he will before too long, he will also know that I am almost always at the convent, giving the illusion that I have virtually abandoned this house along the river. I only pray the Germans do not appropriate Lavender House for their own uses."

"I am sure he knows you are not a nun, Marie. There is little this man does not know or will not know shortly. For that is his mission. The more he knows about us all, the easier he assumes it will be to sort out the chafe from the dross.

"For the time being, the Germans appear content remaining primarily within the town's boundaries and close to Verdun. I hear of no homes this far from the city that they have appropriated for their own living. I do believe, though, if the commandant thought it would upset you in any way, he would have one of his details move in here."

"It is a worry." I did not let on to Henri how much the commandant distressed me. Henri knew, I was sure, that this type of man is only happy when pushing the limits of propriety as he pushed at my boundaries.

During our discussion, I closely observed Henri's reaction to my experiences with the commandant. His response was calmer than I anticipated, and perhaps I was disappointed that he was not more appalled at the commandant's untoward behavior. Almost to the point that, in my frustration, I wondered if my friend truly understood the precarious dance I was attempting.

In the coming days, I noted that the commandant only visited the clinic when there was no evidence of Henri being on the other side of the wall. Nor did he make his presence known when patients were in attendance. He had an uncanny knowledge of when I was alone, which was unnerving.

Bernard told me at our next lunch, as he was leaving my house, that he was sure Reichenbach had men observing many people and places, reporting back to him their comings and goings, but he seemed to be taking a personal interest in the clinic. Henri's jaw merely tightened as we said our *adieux* that day.

I did know that the convent and clinic were now being observed by one or another of Bernard's comrades, appearing to make deliveries, bringing the mail, perhaps acting as a patient now and again. I certainly did not protest their watchful eyes upon us, and neither did the Sisters. Thank goodness the Germans could not see through our walls and into our minds.

CHAPTER 14

STINGING WORDS –
JULY 1940

The day dawned bright and warm, making the short walk to the clinic pleasant, my mind wandering to New York and thoughts of my family. But my heart lurched as I caught sight of the car parked in front of the clinic door. Shortly after the occupation, the commandant had "required" the use of Henri's car, and it seemed he and his driver were everywhere about and around Verdun. Intent on walking casually toward a waiting skirmish of wills, I said a quick prayer to la Vierge Marie and called a clipped bonjour to the commandant and his driver.

"*Guten morgen*, Fräulein Marie. I stopped at a time when I assumed you would not have patients to see. I know you like to get to your clinic early and leave late. What a hardworking and dedicated woman you are."

Detesting his patronizing sneer, I said as pleasantly as possible while unlocking the door, "Yes, I am. And please call me Nurse Durant, and I will call you Commandant Reichenbach. We can talk as I set up for the day."

He followed too closely behind me as I moved quickly through the door toward the safety of my desk, putting it between him and myself. As I bent over to place my worn leather satchel on the floor beside my chair, he took the moment to move to the side of my desk, directly next to me.

He was not a big man, but he manifested an air of embittered entitlement, making his person seem ominously imposing. His well-decorated uniform and tall black boots further lent credence to his aura of power. But I was the taller of us, and when he tucked his hat under his arm, I saw the bald spot atop his head—bare, pink, and vulnerable. He would have been wise to keep his military cap upon that miserable head. I have always enjoyed being tall and never more so than this day standing before this odious man.

"And what questions would you have for me today, Commandant Reichenbach? Or are you perhaps not feeling well?"

"My health is always excellent, Fräulein—or, rather, Nurse Durant, if that is your preference. I am here to ask about a house I understand is a relatively short distance from here and which has been your home for some years. I would ask why you spend most of your nights at the convent rather than returning to your own home."

"As you already understand, I am dedicated to my patients, and traveling miles each day back and forth to an empty house is not my idea of efficiency. Sleeping and eating at the convent allows me to spend more time at the clinic. And I am not one that sees the effort of preparing a meal every day for only myself as a wise use of time. Our cook, Sister Jeanne, on the other hand, is dedicated to the care and feeding of all her Sisters, me included."

As was his custom, the commandant turned and began to inspect the clinic, randomly touching files and items that caught his eye. "How long have you possessed your home? I am told it was passed down to you from your mother?"

"You are a wealth of information, Commandant. Yes, my mother left me the house, and I moved here in the spring of 1920."

"And you have a son? I have not seen him with you," he commented, slowly walking from window to window, peering out as the interrogation continued.

"Oui. He is attending medical school in New York City. He lives with my sister and her family. Why are you asking me these questions, Commandant?"

"A commanding officer has the responsibility to learn all he can about his charges. And since you are one of those, I have a need to know. How often do you return to your home, Mademoiselle?"

"Perhaps once every week or two. Maybe more frequently at this time of the year when the bees are busy in the fields. I enjoy watching them."

He stopped suddenly, his right eye twitching ominously as he spun on his heel to face me. "*Ja*, so I understand. Was it your intent to have such horrible insects around your home?"

"*Mais oui!* My house sits in the middle of nineteen hectares of expansive lavender. Many years ago, the Sisters and I installed hives throughout the property and began an enterprise making honey, lotions, and beeswax candles. There are now more than a hundred active hives."

He turned and resumed pacing stiffly in front of the windows. "I am sure you are aware of the dangers of bees with their deadly stings. Why would you want them surrounding your house? That seems extremely foolish on your part, and dangerous!" Herr Kommandant had become quite agitated during this discussion of my bees.

"Dangerous? The bees are only dangerous to one that might harass them, disturb their hives, or be allergic to stings. The Sisters and I are none of those."

He stopped stock still at the next window, his back to me. "I was stung as a young boy and several times again over the years. I am severely allergic to bees and nearly died from the last incident."

"Then you understand you must be exceedingly careful that you not get stung again, as I am sure your doctor has explained to you."

He spun around impatiently. "I know the dangers, Nurse. But at some point, regardless of your bees, I will inspect your home."

"Certainly, Commandant," I said mildly. "I can be sure to be at the house during a time you specify. The property is alive with thousands upon thousands of bees, several varieties in fact, and some more dangerous than others. You will want to cover yourself carefully with thick clothing and head protection, although I cannot ensure that a bee or two will not find a way to sting your person, regardless of your precautions. They are quite wily and seem to find the smallest of crevices to exert their will."

"And you say the house is empty except for your infrequent visits?"

"Yes. I am perfectly content to spend my days between clinic and convent. The bees are the true occupants of the property, and I choose to let them go about their work in peace."

"I will leave you now to your own work, Nurse Durant." He strode to my desk, picked up a pencil, and deposited it into his trouser pocket before leaving to join his driver.

I hoped the sharpened point would sting his thigh as fiercely as one of my bees.

CHAPTER 15

FATHER O'HARA – JULY 1940

It was a rainy Sunday just after lunch when the commandant appeared at the convent's front door, rapping his knuckles hard against the weathered wood. We all glanced round at one another as Sister Hélène rose and calmly went to see who had come to call. Ronan, who often joined us for a meal, reached over and in one swift motion silenced the radio.

Following Sister Hélène into the kitchen, Commandant Reichenbach approached the table and, standing directly across from me, announced, "Good day, Nurse Durant. I have been meaning to pay your often-talked-about convent a visit, and today worked well with my schedule." With an encompassing wave of his hand, he ordered, "Now please make the introductions."

I rose from my seat, again taking comfort from the fact that I was the taller. No one spoke. The Sisters and Ronan looked calmly at each other, and I let a pause of silence hang in the air as I took a long hard look at the commandant. I did not invite him to sit at our table. Starting to my left and going clockwise round the table, I told him each person's name. "Sister Hélène met you at the door, and next to her is our prioress, Sister Évangéline." Évangéline nodded as the commandant made only brief eye contact with her.

"And this is Sister Marguerite and Sister Béatrice. You already know my assistant, Sister Dominique, and finally, this is Sister Jeanne. Beside her—"

Before I could say Ronan's name, Sister Jeanne jumped from her chair and quickly moved behind Ronan, placing a hand on each of his broad shoulders while saying to the commandant, "And this is Father Ronan O'Hara, sent to us by our Holy Father himself."

I stifled a quick inhalation of surprise, my eyes darting from Ronan to Sister Jeanne and then round the table. Other than myself, no one else seemed the least caught off guard by Sister's declaration proclaiming Ronan to be a Catholic priest. As far as I knew, and what I thought the others at the table knew to be true as well, Ronan O'Hara was an Irishman caught in France by the war; that he was what he told me when he came to my clinic for care, a traveling farrier and journeyman skilled with his hands and out for a walkabout round France. Why was I the only one astonished that he suddenly became a priest sent here specifically by Rome? Henri had told me nothing of this, but I would certainly seek out some answers at the earliest opportunity. Being left in the dark left me feeling vulnerable, frustrated, and somewhat embarrassed.

"Are you the priest of this convent, Father O'Hara?" The commandant's dark eyes drilled the question into Ronan's. It became suddenly apparent the German was here to grill Ronan.

With that easy, broad smile spreading across his comely face, Ronan slowly rose tall from his chair and responded with buoyant confidence, "I am recently here from my home in Ireland, sent by our Holy See to inquire as to the state of the churches in this portion of France, and specially to tend to small convents—like the one here."

"And you are residing here at this convent?"

Ronan gave the commandant a smug smile. "It is cramped quarters enough and cannot hold another soul. I am making my lodgings with my fellow priest and friend, the good Father Aubrey, in Verdun."

"Your purpose here is unclear to me, as there is already a priest in Verdun."

"Aye, aye, Commandant, that is so. But not one who is able to repair crumbling cathedral walls and roof tiles, dig wells, and shoe horses. I am a priest of many skills and quite sought out by churches and convents in need of restoration to their outward temples as well as their spiritual souls."

Sister Jeanne had reclaimed her chair, proudly adding, "Father O'Hara has repaired our leaky roof and is rebuilding our collapsing shed. We are grateful for his assistance, as it has been a long while since the Church has seen fit to send us a representative from the Vatican, much less provide someone who is actually of any practical help."

"I have not heard of traveling priests that were skilled at hard labor. An interesting arrangement, no, Father?"

"This 'arrangement,' as you say, is quite common in the British Isles. The land is hard and many of the churches and convents are rundown after decades, maybe centuries of faithful service. We priests of the north are quite versatile, and the Church does very well using our tradesmen's skills to further the work of our Lord Jesus Christ. My labor still falls under the category of 'priestly duties,' and whilst here, which may be some time now since I cannot return home, I offer my services to the community at large. I am also handy with repairing car engines, so please, do not hesitate should you need assistance with the car you are borrowing from Monsieur Henri."

Ronan had remained standing, and with this verbal barb, he moved a step closer to the commandant, extending his hand forward to shake the German's in dismissal. I had engaged with the commandant times enough that I knew his ire was stirred and he was attempting to tamp down his anger.

With a last hostile look at Ronan, his eye twitching in frustration, the commandant ignored the offered hand, spun round, and headed out the door, calling behind him, "We will talk again, priest." Ronan looked after him, his rakish face sporting that wry grin of his.

With the door firmly closed on the commandant, Sister Évangéline, her smile matching Ronan's own, sprang quickly from her chair, announcing, "I must telephone Father Aubrey! Hopefully he will be most happy to know there is another priest come to town and one who needs to board with him. My gracious!"

CHAPTER 16

MY LAVENDER BEES –
AUGUST 1940

The first time Commandant Reichenbach was delivered to my clinic with multiple stings, it was evident his fear of bees was well founded. He staggered through the door between the long arms of his ever-present minions.

"Nurse, Nurse! Quickly! He is stung many times and his hands and face are so swollen! His eyes may pop from his head!"

I led the frightened men to the plinth table where they deposited their commander onto his back while I placed two pillows under his head to ease his breathing. I asked them to remove themselves to the chairs by the door, and I would get back with them after I completed my examination.

"Can you speak, Commandant?" His response was shallow panting and a red face full of fear. "You must relax and try to calm your breathing. It will not help if you panic but make matters already concerning much worse." I closely examined the many swollen, red sting sites. "Let's see if you can sit up on the edge of the table."

With my help, he managed to raise his upper body and slide his legs over the table's edge. He was staring at me in extreme panic through puffy bloodshot eyes, every muscle in his body tense and contracted. His hands and face were ruddy and swollen from the venom but he was taking in air, and he did not present with nausea or a dangerously elevated pulse rate. I took his blood pressure, noting it was high, but more likely due to fear then anaphylaxis.

After letting him set and attempt to calm himself, his breathing improved; while still labored and heavy, inhalations and exhalations had slowed and the wild look about him had subsided somewhat. I removed his jacket and shirt and bathed his face, hands, and torso in cool water, looking for any remaining barbed stingers. There were several in both hands, four along his face close to his eyes, and several remained lodged in his neck, which I began removing with a small tweezer.

"You are very fortunate, Commandant. While your reaction to the bees' stings has certainly compromised your system, you are not in danger of asphyxiation. At least, not this time. Hold very still while I remove the barbs and tissue they left to you."

Finishing that task, I removed from my apothecary cabinet vinegar, honey, lavender oil, and several strips of muslin and cloth pads. To help him remain calm, I kept my movements slow and measured. I felt I was moving through molasses, pushing through the tasks I knew must be accomplished by a medical provider. My other self, Marie-who-hated-this-man, hovered from above, a disgruntled observer, as I tended my patient.

"Again, I ask you, can you speak now and tell me how you found yourself in such a state? Wherever were you to become such a pin cushion?"

Looking up at me with swollen lids that hooded his blue eyes, he said softly, "At your home, Nurse. That damn house of yours with its damn bees. How you could ever attempt to live in such a despicable place . . ." He paused and continued muttering something in German I couldn't understand.

"Well, thankfully, few people react to bee stings as you do. Were you tromping through the fields looking at the hives?"

"Of course not! Do you think me a fool? *Mein Gott!* I was merely walking up the steps to your front door. The devils set upon me instantly, and I was swelling before I could get back to my car and be driven straight here."

"And why, knowing full well that bee toxin literally threatens your life, would you decide to approach my home surrounded by active hives in hectares of lavender in the middle of summer? That action certainly seems like something only a fool would do. Hold still while I saturate the sting sites with vinegar. It draws out the toxin."

He winced and cursed in German as I liberally applied the pungent liquid. I let him sit and stew in his wounds until the skin dried. I then observed him for another thirty minutes, until his breathing normalized and the swelling in his throat subsided. The swelling in his body had not extended and, checking his pulse and blood pressure, his vital signs were now within normal range. He was a fortunate fool but, most likely, would not be if stung again.

"Did I not tell you the house is uninhabited and the fields the provenance of the bees? Why would you take such risk, Commandant?" I asked while applying a thick layer of lavender honey to his hands, face, and neck. He looked like a monster but smelled wonderful. I almost laughed out loud at the dissonance. How I detested this man and yet, the nurse in me betrayed my base instincts of hatred. I felt my own breathing slow and experienced reluctant relief, knowing my patient was now out of danger. Such a dichotomy.

I glanced round the beautiful tapestried privacy screens at the two young soldiers fidgeting in the chairs. Both, having been stung several times as well, were rubbing and scratching away at their hands and faces; however, there was no evidence of any distress other than some swelling and discomfort. They could sit there and scratch.

I handed my patient a glass of water, instructing him to take a few small sips so I could assess his swallow.

"I am not thirsty. Just finish what you need to do and let me leave," he said, pushing the glass away. We shared a look of equal frustration, but I placed the glass on the counter.

"I will give you additional strips of muslin and the jar of lavender honey to take with you," I said, wrapping a thin layer of muslin twice around each of his swollen hands. "Apply more honey before you go to sleep. In the morning, dab the stings with the lavender oil I give you, let it sit for ten minutes, then reapply the bandages and honey if needed."

"What if I wake in the night and can't breathe? Or my eyes swell shut?"

"That would certainly remind you of the fact that you need keep a great distance from bees. I do not think your symptoms will extend to additional swelling but do not scratch the sting sites, and especially do not scratch or touch your eyes. You can soak your hands and face in cool water, but do not pick at the sites. And for God's sake, stay away from bees!"

"Again, woman, I am no imbecile. This was an accident that could not be avoided and occurred in the line of duty. With my responsibilities come risks as well, and I accept them as a part of war."

"And will your family accept and understand you were killed in the war by a swarm of bees?"

"Ha! I have no family. The Spanish flu took my wife and two children and, therefore, my only loyalty is to my country and my Führer."

With great effort and injured pride, he got down from the table and walked stiffly around the privacy screens to his men, his limp more prominent than ever. He stopped and turned to me before reaching the door. "Thank you, Nurse Durant," he said, placing a pile of German currency atop Sister Dominique's desk. "I suppose I am grateful for your care."

"I suppose you should be, Commandant Reichenbach."

CHAPTER 17

RATIONING –
OCTOBER 1940–SPRING 1941

As further and more restrictive anti-Semitic laws continued to be enforced, decreeing that Jews could not work as doctors, journalists, professors, or teachers and could not own businesses, our own town of Verdun was severely impacted. Classrooms were left without teachers, long-time family-owned businesses closed, shops and offices suddenly empty—the town took on just a semblance of itself as citizens and friends disappeared. And where did these ostracized ones go? We heard half-truths and half-lies and only asked the question out of our inability to comprehend the truth, the reality that though we were all suffering from the occupation, none knew yet the extent of the horror and suffering of our missing neighbors.

We gleaned any accurate news of the war's progress from clandestine listenings to the BBC, passing news word of mouth across one household to another as a radio operator was able to dial in London. We also learned firsthand the abysmal state of life in Paris as residents brought news after fleeing the city in hopes of finding food from rural farms.

Rural areas became important food sources for the urban populations. Many traveled from the larger cities on "*trains des haricots*," vegetable trains, searching the farms and gardens of small villages, such as ours along the River Meuse, scouring for anything fresh and edible to take back to their families. While I did not hear of anyone starving, I did see scores of undernourished people as they appeared at the convent or my clinic.

The system of rationing implemented by the Germans was based on coupons. Ration books were issued with coupons for food items and clothes, textiles, coal, petrol—everything that was life sustaining. By the spring of 1941, the food shortages were staggering and found people waiting long hours in endless lines. Often, once you arrived at the front of the line, there was nothing left. And if anything did remain in the way of food, it was frequently not fit to eat. These coupons became useless slips of paper, daily reminders of all that was lost and the inability to change any of it.

It was said the urban citizens talked obsessively about food and of how and where to find it. They spoke of violent riots in Paris as desperate people fought for a place in the queues, fearing there would be no food left when it was their turn. As punishment for these uprisings, the Germans would ban the distribution of staples like potatoes or flour, leaving the residents in even greater straits.

Over the next two years, young French men were conscripted into the German military by the hundreds of thousands as laborers, the "*Service du travail obligatoire*," resulting in fewer local farmers to raise crops sufficient to feed the populace of France. What commercial crops we did have were prioritized to feed the German war effort—our occupiers.

Our men were sent to Germany to work their factories and mines, to see first to the needs of the German army and the German people. Women, old men, and children became the backbone of occupied France. These staunch souls kept our factories running and businesses operating as they struggled to feed their families and attend to the difficult realities of life controlled by the enemy. Even then, most of our manufactured goods and merchandise were exported. Eventually, leather became so scarce that people began repairing their shoes using wooden soles, canvas tops, and even paper. Our clothes were patched and repatched, and fabric was almost impossible to come by, even enough to make repairs or alterations. Our hungry children grew more waiflike and ragged. We did the best we could with what little we had.

Sugar and sweets of any kind, as well as coffee and other staples, were deemed "unrationables" and could only be obtained by the wealthy through the thriving black market, "*le marché noir.*" Unless you had a connection with *le marché noir*, which many did, or were able to grow enough on your own to feed yourself and your family, larders were lean.

From time to time, Henri asked if we could spare a portion of our hidden honey and candles for him to use as barter. He would soon return with items we knew were not acquired from any store in Verdun. The Sisters and I did not question where they came from. We were grateful that, along with the jars of canned goods from our gardens and animals, these infrequent added rations helped us sustain ourselves.

The Sisters canned throughout the summer and fall, lining deep, wide wooden shelves with air-tight glass jars, hidden as best they could in the dark recesses of the cool cellar of the convent. Row upon row of gleaming glass stood unseen, ready to be doled out as food or barter throughout the long winters and cool springs. We planted early, late, and continually. Our diet was usually much the same as the rabbits and chickens, and only occasionally did we sacrifice one of our animals, when real meat protein was deemed absolutely necessary. We were fortunate to have prolific hens and ate so many eggs we thought we might turn yellow. It was the brightest part of our lives during those difficult years, the fact that we could all nurture one another in every loving way possible.

CHAPTER 18

INTIMIDATION – MAY 1941

The commandant continued his impromptu early morning appearances before my clinic began its daily operation but lately unaccompanied and always knocking once upon the clinic's door, one short rap before his hand was turning the latch. His visits felt clandestine, as though he did not want others to know where he was. Upon hearing the twice or thrice weekly knocks upon my door, I merely called out, *"Entrez!"* and remained at whatever task I was about. My body always braced involuntarily, and I slowed my breathing and collected my emotions before he entered, striding loudly across the floor.

"You seem to make your way out of town earlier and earlier these past weeks, Commandant. And what inquiries might you have for me in the darkness before sunrise? Surely they must be of an urgent nature to appear so early."

"Do not be snide, Nurse. It is neither necessary nor becoming. I could just as easily take you into Verdun for questioning."

As was his usual during his interrogations of me, he began his pacing round the clinic, touching and fingering this and that, often grasping one of my sterile instruments or patient files, appearing to closely examine it before setting it down again.

"What is your relationship to your neighbor Henri? Is he a relative or merely your lover?"

"Henri? Henri is a friend, a friend to us all. I have known him since my arrival in Meuse in 1920."

"You did not answer the questions. Is he not the father of your illegitimate son? The son you sent off to America?"

"Ha! Why do you spend your time conjuring stories, Commandant? It is not necessary nor becoming."

He kept walking round and round, pausing before whatever caught his eye. He stopped in front of the tapestried privacy screens, running his right hand slowly across the intricate stitches of beautiful cranes and flowers, the thick silk of the fabric changing hues with each brush of his intrusive stroking. I watched his cloying hands and swallowed hard through clenched jaws.

He walked over to where I stood between the corner of my desk and the end of the screens and stopped squarely in front of me. "And where is your son's father?"

"He is dead, just as your wife and children are. Dead and gone in another war."

His arm flew up, palm outstretched, and holding myself firmly, I prepared for his slap to my face. But I was caught off guard when he paused at my cheek and began stroking it with the fingers of his right hand—rough, coarse fingers. I didn't flinch at that, didn't give him the satisfaction, but instead wondered what else he must do to have the hands of a farmer.

Then his hand slid under my chin and rested there. His foul touch coursed through my body, and I shivered in disgust. He smiled. I cast my eyes down and tightly held my counsel. If I looked at him, I would surely vomit hate upon his ghastly green uniform.

He brought his fingers to my hair and slowly removed a pin. A thick lock fell across my bent brow and into my eyes. The veil of hair served to hide my look of loathing as anger burned inside me.

I looked up and tucked my hair behind my left ear, seething. "How dare you! Take your hands from my person and step away from me immediately."

"It is fortunate for your neighbors that not everyone is as belligerent as you, Nurse Durant."

"Belligerent? I find my responses justified in light of your insolence."

GAIL NOBLE-SANDERSON · 91

"I would like to think you, as a nurse, to be a more genteel woman than what you exhibit. But these are difficult times, and I suppose I can be generous. You will become more content when you merely accept that we are here to stay. This *is* your life now."

"We were perfectly content before you ever arrived."

Pocketing my hairpin, he looked at me with threatening eyes. "Do you imagine your small protests matter to me?"

"I do not care what matters to you. Just because you are here does not in any way diminish who we are. We but wait patiently for the time when all of you are gone and we may get on with our lives."

"Was your son's father a Jew? Is that why you sent him away, because he is a Jew?"

"And now you insult my family? Leave, before I grab one of my scalpels and slit your throat."

His eyes narrowed and he smiled. A vile, smug smile. "You do entertain me, Fräulein. Our visits are much more satisfying than my usual conversations."

My hair fallen forward again without my hairpin, he reached up and tucked it behind my ear then turned and walked out the door, closing it quietly behind him. Or maybe he closed it loudly and I could not hear over the ferocious beating of my heart. How tempted I was to gather a few of my bees and have them ready to sting the next time he came to call. This sorry excuse of a man deserved nothing less.

CHAPTER 19

LOSS – APRIL 1942

D eath sucks the life from the living as well as the dead. Your departed takes your soul with them when they pass. And the air—the air is sucked from your lungs and there is no way to breathe. Gasping—gasping only. No breath to continue living. And no words. There are no words to say and no words to describe the anguish of loss after losing one you love. But there are feelings. Feelings of remorse, feelings of anguish that roll over and over you as tidal waves, consuming you in flames of fire, laying you bare and naked before the truth of death as fear-tinged adrenaline roars through your body. And all you want is to die as well, to die and escape the pain.

The letter arrived in April, delivered by someone I did not know who found me early morning at the clinic. The wrinkled envelope was worn, as though it had been transferred between many pockets before finally landing in my own trembling hands. The musty smell from the paper lingered on my fingertips as I gently placed the missive on my clinic desk. Encased within the envelope, I could faintly see a slip of yellow laid upon a page of black type. I knew instinctively its contents held no good news. It was postmarked "King's College, London, England." But the handwriting was not his, and I knew as well that he was serving with the British Army in a hospital in Singapore.

I decided to take myself and the letter to my convent room where I would be undisturbed. The letter would not be read here, here in this place where Tanvir and I found each other that day he arrived so unexpectedly. We loved each other here on my old creaky plinth table—our bodies a sacrifice, an offering of compensation for all the pain we bore, both our own and for all those we had cared for. No, I would not read it here. He would always be here, with me, alive in this place where we spent precious time as colleagues, friends, and lovers.

Picking up the letter and depositing it into my own pocket, I set off the short distance up the hill toward the Sisters. I did not know if I could make the easy climb today. My heavy heart was an exceptional burden.

I silently entered through the convent's front door, immediately turned right, and then left, just before the chapel doors, to my room. I sat stiffly on my cot, tears running down my face onto the envelope in my hands, and wondered why, oh why, was I crying. But I knew. I knew. And so steeled my broken heart to bear the news.

March 1942
La Clinique Meuse
Nurse Marie Durant
Verdun, France

Madame Durant,

It is with great sorrow that I must convey to you sad news. Our mutual friend and respected colleague, Dr. Tanvir Singh, was killed this last 14 February during the horrific attack by the Japanese army on Alexandra Hospital, Singapore.

The shelling began in the morning, followed by the soldiers storming the hospital in the early afternoon hours. They massacred patients, physicians, nurses, and staff. More than two hundred were lost over the days of the siege on this safe-zone hospital. Dr. Singh and his surgical team were in the operating theatre at the time of the initial attack, and there our friend suffered his death at the end of a Japanese bayonet. I pray his death was swift.

Dr. Singh shared with me his great admiration for your work, both during WWI and now, in your clinic in Meuse. He was very fond of you and asked that if I heard any news of him that he was himself unable to send, I should please pass it on to you.

I trust that somehow, despite the great chaos of these days, my letter finds its way into your hands. May your good work persist and sustain you during these difficult times.

Sincere condolences,
Dr. Benjamin Hooser
King's College, School of Medicine
London, England

Two full months of not having known was now heaped atop the guilt and grief on the other side of knowing. Guilt that I had not been grieving these past two months but instead went on with my life, my wretched life full of worry and worry and worry. All our wretched lives full of this war that made our stomachs and souls ache with emptiness and fear. The hopelessness and helplessness of it all—the humiliating occupation, the terror of every day, the futility of yet another war and inevitable loss. And now this—this unbearable reality.

The fourteenth of February. My dreams in February had been angst-ridden and fierce. I would wake up shaking, sweat clinging to my cold body. Those night terrors did not consist of visions but sounds—screams of fear and suffering. The same moans I used to hear in my dreams and from my own person those years ago from another war had returned to torment my sleep. I felt the pain of death in every fast, shallow breath. The pain of others came to me superimposed onto my own past wounds and scars, making it all real again. My soul was tortured as these dark nights became darker weeks and blacker months. I knew something dreadful had happened.

And by day, the Germans continued to ravage our lives. People disappeared, whole families gone—removed from their homes, from our streets and city as though they had never been a part of us. Verdun was being depleted of life in all ways. Our bodies hungry and made more so by the daily ritual of standing for hours in long lines for meager rations. Our spirits numb and defeated. Our minds staggering in denial at all that was happening as news of continued defeat again and again reached our disbelieving ears.

And now, swallowing the devastating news of Tanvir's death delivered to me in this jagged, cutting letter, boring its terrible news whole into my fractured soul, I felt a righteous anger ignite and begin to rise up. The word "resistance" briefly burned bright in my mind. I knew Henri, Bernard, and others were fighting clandestine battles—ones of duplicity and cunning and filled with great risk. But what was left to risk? What more had I to lose? What might we save? I felt no fear.

Needing to read the letter but once, I folded it and slid it back into the worn envelope. But the letter caught and I looked down. Inside the envelope was the yellow paper. An origami crane. Those I knew so well and kept as mementos of each time Tanvir and I were together. And now, one last gift from my beloved friend. Unfolding the crane and lifting the paper to my face, I could smell the faint aroma of him, cloves and cinnamon and cardamom. Overcome by a great malaise, I lay down upon my bed with my sorrow, tucking the paper crane under my blouse and gently against my left breast where it would warm, the scent of him lasting the endless night with me.

CHAPTER 20

CONSOLATION – APRIL 1942

After three days of her self-imposed solitude, I managed to persuade the Sisters to allow me entrance into Marie's grief. I insisted she had languished in her isolation long enough, and if she needed help stepping back into life, I was more than willing to assist. Besides, she was needed by her patients and I was losing patience as well.

My sharp rap to her room's heavy wood door was followed by the loud answer of silence.

"Marie, I need to talk with you and you need to eat. And you need a bath. I can smell your melancholy through the cracks of the door."

"Go away, Henri. I need nothing other than for you to leave me alone."

"You have had three days of sorrow, ma chère. The terrible loss of Tanvir cannot be followed by your own demise."

There was no sound on the other side of the door, no attempt to rise up among the living.

"Go away, Henri. I am fine—just very, very tired."

"You are more than tired. You have not slept or eaten. Between grief and fatigue you cannot possibly take care of yourself. I'm going to open the door, ma chère."

I slowly opened her door and stepped inside. The room was dark and full of loss, the air thick with the smell of desolation. As I approached her bed, she turned her body to the wall, as though she could disappear. Not wanting to frighten her, I stepped with quiet footfalls and knelt at the side of her bed, attempting to find her among the tangle of covers and quilts. I felt her forehead and found it too warm to the touch. Mon Dieu, she was truly sick with her grief. The Sisters should not have left her alone for so long—and neither should I.

A glass filled with yesterday's water sat on the small wooden stand beside her bed. She needed to sit up and drink. Freeing her from her cocoon, I placed my left arm around her thin shoulders and my right under her knees and raised her to sitting, leaning her back against the bare white wall behind her bed. Her eyes were closed, and her head fell to her chest.

"For God's sake, Marie, open your eyes! You are not leaving us today nor the next. We are all too selfish to let you go."

"And I am too selfish to stay, Henri. For all my brave talk of hope, I am a tired coward. Just let me go. Let me go."

"Be quiet and drink." I held the glass to her lips, forcing them apart, spilling the water down her front as well as into her mouth. She took three small swallows, choking on the liquid before closing her mouth tight. She still had not opened her eyes.

"You are being selfish and stubborn. Leaving your friends is one thing but how can you desert your patients? How can you turn your back on the clinic you worked for so very long to secure? Would it not be more honoring to Tanvir's memory to get up and carry on than to languish here? Your skills are of more service than your needless death. You don't need hope today, ma chère, just courage enough to put your feet to the floor."

"So much death, Henri. Too much. And I cannot do this anymore. I have no courage."

"I have courage for both of us. Open your eyes and look at me, Marie. . . . Marie . . . Just be courageous enough to trust me. We will find our way again, as we always have."

I held the glass of water once more to her lips but waited until she opened her eyes and saw me before tipping the glass for her to drink. Her eyes were empty—hollow orbs filled with hopelessness that frightened me to the point that I had to force myself to hold her gaze. Giving her shoulders a firm grasp and a smile of encouragement, I got up and fully opened the door, meeting the wide, anxious looks of the Sisters.

"Sister Jeanne, Marie is ready to eat. Can you place a small bowl of soup at her place in the kitchen and I will bring her out. Please call Sister Dominique and have her come assess our friend. While she is eating, please have her bed changed and fresh clothes laid out, her day clothes, and she will need to be bathed before you help her dress."

They all nodded and took off in haste, each to an assigned task to resurrect our friend. I eased Marie's legs over the side of the bed, planting her feet firmly to the floor, and prompted her to stand.

"You know, Henri. There is nothing wrong with me that death won't cure."

"Ah, how wrong you are. The truth is, there is everything wrong with you that only the love of your friends can cure. At least be gracious enough to accept our consolations."

With my arm around her, I half carried her to the kitchen and sat her in her usual chair looking out to the gardens. Sister Jeanne had ladled out bowls of soup for us both. I fell heavily onto the seat beside her, forcing the meal into my own mouth as I encouraged Marie to eat hers.

She needed a reason to live, a point of hope on which to focus. It was time now to try and save those we could and restore a sense of purpose to our shattered lives. Marie was never more alive than when she had a cause.

I would have preferred nothing more than to have lain down beside her, turning our faces to one another and drifting off together, away from all the madness. No one understood her suffering more than I. For as she could not bear the death of Tanvir, I could not bear a world without her.

CHAPTER 21

RESTORATION – APRIL 1942

Five days following Henri's rescue of my despondent self, I hesitantly returned to the clinic. My sorrow was mingled with guilt as I saw patient after patient who had been worrying over my "illness." Their expressions of condolence regarding Tanvir were kind but not welcome. I could not survive every day with constant reminders of what had been lost, not just to me but to so many—his family, his friends and students, the realm of medicine and research. Death is far reaching and leaves a wide hole in the world.

Henri insisted I spend the night that week in his home rather than returning to the convent. He wanted to "keep a close eye" on me. He instructed Sister Dominique to end my patient appointments at five in the afternoon, at which time I would finish up my notes and filing, say *bonsoir* to Sister, and then cross the threshold into Henri's domain. He always had a meal waiting for us, wine on the table, and a fire in the stove. I'd always known he traded on the black market, but I had every reason not to ask. Henri had always been a man with many secrets and never more so than during wartime.

His tender care for my wounded soul allowed me to maintain a semblance of sanity. I did not have much fortitude for life, but I did have enough of a conscience to realize I could not desert my friends as Tanvir had deserted me. I would not be a cause for such angst. By the end of the week, fed on milk and meat, bread and sweets, rich red wine, and the balm of quiet conversation and dreamless sleep, Henri generously stoked me back to life.

This was at least the third time I had survived the unbearable—the first war with my physical and mental wounds from the devastation in the battlefield, followed next by my despondent and lonely move to Meuse as my beloved Papa and Solange left for America, and now this brutality of yet another war—the accumulation of loss upon loss. Henri assured me this would be the last of the unbearable times.

"I realize I owe you my very life, Henri. Time and again you have been my rock. But at this moment, I have only this altered version of myself to present to you and the world. I resent that I am among the living, ashamed that I sit here in comfort while so many lay dying and dead. And I don't know where he is."

"It must be very difficult for you not to know if Tanvir's body was recovered and sent home to India. For you not to be able to share your sorrow with those you both knew, and not be able to communicate with Félix, letting him know his friend and mentor is gone."

"It is a tormented, solitary grief. I do not know if shared sorrow is somehow more bearable or the accumulation of so much shared sorrow would be overwhelming. My experiences were brief interludes in Tanvir's life. Only he and I knew the extent of our relationship, our history, our hope for the world's restoration after the war, for medical miracles that were almost a reality but for the war. Always the damned wars."

"Why do you assume those who love you did not know of your deep affection toward Dr. Singh? It was certainly apparent to me and, I'm sure, to the Sisters. We all respected your privacy, your perceived need for the relationship to appear collegial rather than personal. I don't think Félix knew of your deep mutual regard, but really Marie, you do your friends a disservice thinking we did not see your joy."

"Perhaps I felt protective of what I had never experienced before this relationship with a man. And I was concerned that I would cause you pain. If I thought others did not know, then I did not need to feel any sense of guilt."

"While we can't share your memories, ma chère Marie, we all came to admire and respect Tanvir. It could not have been easy for him to leave all he had here and return to India."

I got up from the table and went to the window, staring out at nothing, perhaps dreading the answer to my question. "And you were not jealous?"

"I did not say I was not envious that he was the object of your affections, having hoped for so long those feelings would grow in my direction. But I understood. I could never begrudge you happiness, and you certainly have no reason to feel any sense of guilt or disloyalty. Truly, I am very sorry for your loss. He was a fine physician and a good man."

I was slowly walking the perimeter of his front room, much as the commandant did in my clinic. "Yes, he was all those things—greatly loved and respected. Much as you are, my friend."

With a sad, slow smile, Henri stood and walked to the kitchen, leaving the remnants of conversation much as the crumbs of our meal lay scattered across our cold plates.

CHAPTER 22

PHILIPPA – APRIL 1942

"**B**onjour, Nurse Durant. I know we are early for our nine o'clock appointment." called Félicité as she ushered her bent-at-the-middle friend, Eugénie, through the clinic door.

"Madame Eugénie, what has happened to you? Please, sit and be comfortable," said Sister Dominique.

"Merci, but I can neither sit nor stand nor walk without discomfort! Nurse, wherever are you?"

Upon hearing their arrival and the sounds of concern, I finished washing my hands and calmly stepped round the screen toward the front where the three women stood.

"You have injured yourself, Eugénie?" Taking her arm, I slowly guided her to the examining table, Félicité close on her other side.

"Well, it isn't for lack of trying to take care of it myself, I'll tell you that."

"What exactly are you trying to take care of?"

The tall woman remained silent for many seconds before Félicité chimed in. "Tell her, Eugénie. She is a medical professional, and in moments like these you can't think of her as anything else."

Realizing Eugénie was embarrassed by whatever confession lay at her lips, I stood her beside the table, which she gratefully leaned against before taking a deep sigh and telling me as she kept her eyes on the wall.

"I am a strong and hearty person and not one to complain. However, of late I have had digestive difficulties to such a degree that I am plagued both by boils and constipation." Looking at me now, in a great rush of confidence, words tumbled from her mouth. "And I am bleeding, Marie. Every time I push now to unsuccessfully evacuate my bowels, there is blood, great burning, and excruciating pain. We have tried everything we know to do, to no gain. And with company arriving tomorrow it is imperative that I be my usual efficient self. There. Now it is up to you, Nurse Durant, to please repair me to myself." She was close to tears, and Félicité had tears running down her own face.

"I want you to undress from your waist down and then Sister Dominique and I will help you onto the table. I strongly suspect you are suffering from hemorrhoids, which can be extremely painful. Do you want Félicité to help you get undressed?"

They both nodded as I stepped once again round the screen and over to Sister's desk, where she held Eugénie's chart toward me with a kind smile upon her face. I smiled in return, listening to the muffled voices of the two friends, returning to them only when Félicité appeared, letting me know Eugénie was ready to be examined.

They had gotten her onto the table and Félicité had covered her with the clean linen cloth. Upon examination, she presented with both internal and external hemorrhoids, significantly large and excessively inflamed, the bleeding coming from the internal inflammation. Her stomach was distended and solid. She was also tender under her breastbone and elicited a small cry of discomfort when I palpated her lower abdomen. My stethoscope registered no abdominal sounds. All was ominously silent in that regard.

"When did you last go to the bathroom?"

"It must be almost five days now, and not for lack of trying, I might add."

"Besides water, have you eaten or drunk anything in the last two days?"

"Of course not. Why would I do that?"

"I am concerned you have a bowel blockage, Eugénie, either from severe prolonged constipation or some other issue. I am going to administer an enema to assist your body in discharging what it is so determined to hold on to. Have you ever had an enema before?"

"Of course not. Why would I?"

I smiled at her fearful, forceful self, patted her hand, and said, "You will feel even more pressure in your abdomen as the warm water enters, and even though you will want to push it out, I want you to contract your muscles and hold the water inside as long as possible. Longer than you think you possibly could. Can you do that?"

"Of course I can. Why would I not be able to do that?"

Patting her again, I called to Sister to prepare the water bag and set-up. I then had Félicité join us, explaining the procedure again, reassuring them both, with more confidence than I felt, that Eugénie would feel much better shortly.

After turning the clinic sign to "Closed" and spending the next two hours gently and not-so-gently palpating, infusing warm water, and using my speculum to assist Eugénie's body, she was significantly relieved—though sore and with some additional bleeding. I applied ointment, Sister gave her tea, and Félicité held Eugénie's hand. I was in no hurry to have her leave but kept her lying on the table with cool compresses of lavender tea and honey applied to the afflicted area. When she insisted on sitting and another cup of tea, I kept her engaged in conversation, delaying their departure until I could again reexamine and listen for bowel sounds.

"You said you had company arriving tomorrow. Whom are you expecting?"

"My niece, Philippa. She was born here but has lived with her mother in Reims for many years. Now that her mother has recently passed, she is coming for a visit, perhaps for a much-extended time. Both my brother, Bernard, and I have encouraged her to think about moving closer to us. Especially in these terrible times and knowing we are the only family left to her."

"You have a brother living here named Bernard?"

"Why of course, dear. You know Bernard well. It is his daughter who is arriving tomorrow."

I stopped abruptly, turned to her in consternation, and said, "Your brother is Bernard? Bernard Schultz? Henri's friend Bernard? Rose's husband Bernard?"

"Why yes, Marie. Of course. Why ever are you so amazed at this? It cannot be news."

But it most certainly was news. How this lady of refinement could be related to blustering, gruff Bernard did not seem remotely possible.

"And you say he has a daughter? A daughter named Philippa, and she is arriving here tomorrow by train from Reims?" I continued to stare incredulously at this woman of very advanced years, wondering how Bernard, most likely in his fifties, could have such an older sibling and a daughter as well. And why was I never told any of this? A daughter living with her mother meant either his first wife had not really died, as had been intimated to me, or that she wasn't his first wife.

I pulled my thoughts back to my patient. "How are you feeling, Eugénie? Let's walk you round the room a bit before I take one more look. Perhaps you could tell me more about your niece's situation. I did not know Bernard had a daughter but assumed his first wife passed many years ago, leaving him with no children, just his sheep."

"Oh, Marielle wasn't his first wife. Patricia was his first wife. I could tell you that marriage wasn't going to last. She left Bernard when Philippa was two, and they both packed off to Reims, where she was from. Philippa is the only good thing to come from that union.

"But when he met Marielle, well, that changed everything. She certainly was the love of his life. And those foul sheep of his. You'd think those bleating creatures were the only ones God ever created and He created them especially for my brother. I admit he has always been somewhat of a disappointment to me, never completing school after the war, but just returning to his wife and sheep. After she passed, he was so desolate I thought he might leave us."

"I took care of one of Bernard's pregnant ewes on a cold Christmas Eve many years ago. He was especially relieved, we all were, when the small twin lambs were safely born. Those twins were our Christmas gifts that year. Henri and your brother stayed at the convent and had dinner with the Sisters and myself. It is a fond memory."

"That sounds like Bernard. Thinking nothing of interrupting someone's holiday. Our mother had him very late in life. As late as can be, as she died during the birth. Forty-five years of age is far too old to birth a baby. She and father tried for many years, and many miscarriages later, Bernard was born. My mother was but seventeen when I was born. Bernard is my very, very younger brother. He was headstrong and independent from the moment he opened his mouth with a fierce cry. I raised him with father as best I could, attempting to direct him toward an education and a taste for refinement. Ha! That certainly never came to pass," she said, sitting herself back onto the plinth table with greater ease so I could conduct one last examination.

One more hour, four cups of tea, and two successful purging procedures later, I was feeling confident and greatly reassured there was no internal blockage. I sent her home with instructions and ointment, the same ones I always gave to her brother, and Sister Dominique scheduled her for a follow-up appointment the next week.

Upon closing the door behind the two women, I told Sister Dominique to take an hour and have her midday meal at the convent with the others. I would set things to right before our two o'clock appointment. I needed time alone to process what Eugénie had shared and sort through my feelings. Her surprising revelations greatly disturbed me. Not so much because Bernard was her brother but because I didn't know. All this time. I felt feelings of betrayal, as though Henri and Bernard had been lying to me by omission.

And I was angry. Truth be told, it felt quite good to be angry with someone other than the Germans. And it seemed I had been angry with Henri about something or the other for the last eighteen years we had been friends, so my righteous indignation over Henri's withholding Eugénie and Bernard's siblingship felt well placed and provided an interesting distraction. It was much easier on the soul to be frustrated with ones you loved than ones you hated.

I pondered also the stark differences between Eugénie and Bernard. There was no discernable likeness in physical characteristics, although both did share a strong and opinionated disposition—Bernard in his blustery, coarse personality while Eugénie demonstrated a refined, self-confident comportment. The only resemblance I clearly saw between brother and sister was their predisposition for "arse boils," as Bernard called them.

CHAPTER 23

REVELATIONS – APRIL 1942

Early in the morning, just as Sister Dominique and I arrived at la Clinique Meuse, Henri knocked firmly from his side of the door.

"Come in, Henri."

"Bonjour, Marie, Sister Dominique. Marie, might you spare a few minutes before you begin with your patients and have tea with me?"

I looked up quickly, taking in the soft voice and slow cadence of Henri's words, knowing I was being *summoned* to have morning tea with my friend. I rose from my desk and, giving Sister Dominique a knowing look, crossed the threshold into his home. Bernard was there as well, pacing round the kitchen table like a caged animal.

I was becoming alarmed. "What is happening, Henri?"

"Father O'Hara has been taken to Gestapo headquarters in Verdun. Yesterday morning, the Germans went to the cathedral and took Ronan into custody. Father Aubrey called me immediately, and I have been doing what is possible to have him released, including speaking with Reichenbach."

Henri motioned for Bernard to sit down as I began pouring tea into our cups. I served slowly and methodically, taking in this unexpected turn of events and attempting to relieve Bernard of any more angst than he was already demonstrating. "And what did you learn?" I said, handing Henri his cup.

"Ronan can produce no official paperwork verifying he is here as a representative of the Catholic church. Reichenbach is making the charge that he is, in reality, a subversive. A member of the French Resistance and therefore committing crimes against Germany."

"And does the commandant have evidence of these accusations?"

"He needs no evidence to lay guilt upon those he oppresses! It is to his benefit when people can produce no legal paperwork—allows him to throw a great number into custody, thereby showing he is rooting out subversives. I'm sure it looks impressive on his mandatory reports to his superiors. Securing Ronan rids him of one more strong man he cannot strong-arm."

"Did you see Ronan? How is our friend faring?"

"Our cynically optimistic Father O'Hara remains in his usual good spirits and seems not the least concerned about what he says is a 'temporary imposition.' I think rather he is finding it an enlightening experience but one we need to remove him from immediately, before they throw him onto a train headed to a labor camp and we never see him again."

Bernard rose from the table, pounding his fists one into the other and again taking up his pacing. "I told you we should have killed the bastard! I will do it! He'll never even see it coming." Neither Henri nor I made comment to Bernard's gathering storm.

"And what happens now? How did you leave it with the commandant?"

"I expressed my sincere regret that an innocent man, a man of the Church no less, should be charged so unfairly, expressing confidence that the omniscient commandant would see past the error and release the good father.

"Reichenbach asked what it was to me what happened to the man, why was I so concerned. I made light of it, telling him the Sisters had sent me to ask for his release and that the work Father O'Hara performed was less work I had to do. That the industrious priest kept us all in good order, reminding the commandant he himself took advantage of the father's skills, including multiple repairs to my automobile that he drove so harshly up and down the uneven roads. I also reminded him that the Church would not look kindly upon the imprisonment of one sent from the Vatican.

"I left him saying that I knew of no activities that would in any way constitute subversion. As far as I knew, Germany was not at war with Ireland, and Germany was not at war with the Catholic church, and the commandant must have others he can prove of misdeeds. And I reminded him that detaining Father O'Hara was a waste of his good time when he should be worrying about his weekly portion of borscht at the café. I then wondered aloud if it was perhaps the same borscht recipe his Reichenbach grandparents perhaps shared with my own Reichenbach *grands-parents*.

"As this reference to his questionable ancestry registered across his face, I saw fear mingled with deep contempt before he dismissed me with a curt wave of his hand, saying, 'You are correct in that I certainly have more urgent matters to attend to than listening to feeble pleas from feeble men such as yourself.' He began to limp away but turned back and said, 'And as to you and I having any relatives past or present, be assured that is completely impossible and, therefore, not to be mentioned to me again.'

"Taking my cue to leave, I nodded in his direction but sent one more piece of information toward his back. I told him I had some evidence, held by others, that we indeed had a probable shared lineage that might prove an interesting read for his superiors should anything happen to Father O'Hara, anyone associated with the convent, including Marie, or myself.

"He stopped abruptly, faced me again, and said, 'I do not know whether to admire your bravery in insulting me or to immediately throw you in with the Catholic for your insubordination.' Eye twitching madly and red in the face, he turned and limped away as quickly as he could manage."

"And now we do what," I asked.

"We wait, as Father Aubrey is currently making an official complaint on behalf of the Catholic church and on behalf of his fellow Irishman."

"You think the Irish can help under these circumstances?"

"Ronan assured me he was born and raised in Ireland, attending seminary there before being sent to France, where he has visited and served the Church on and off for the past thirty years, mostly in the Reims area. I am hoping that, despite any evidence, Ronan is indeed a verified and vested priest. The commandant will be given a formal written complaint on the church's letterhead and Father Aubrey's own affirmation that Ronan is who he says he is. Along with this formal written protest, Father Aubrey is planning on confirming to the commandant that when he retires in two years, Father O'Hara is slated to become the cathedral's next priest. And perhaps Reichenbach will hear my words again when he has his favored borscht as he contemplates my threat of sending up my information. We can only wait."

I had heated more water and motioned restless Bernard to again sit down before I poured it into the teapot. We all needed to keep our wits about us, and I voiced as much as we then sat silently drinking our tea, me sending a fervent prayer to la Vierge Marie.

"Do you really have such information, Henri? That the commandant could be Jewish?"

Henri merely shrugged his shoulders and raised his eyebrows, smiling wryly in a way I knew indicated nothing more would be said of the matter. Three days later, we received news from Father Aubrey that Ronan, because of his status as a Catholic priest, had been released but would be kept under close surveillance. For now, Ronan was lying low at the cathedral, assisting Father Aubrey in affairs of the Church.

Along with efforts on the part of Father Aubrey, I had no doubt Henri's name-dropping had proved a powerful incentive swaying the commandant's decision to release our good Father O'Hara. And I knew that Henri was safe— for now, anyway. I allowed myself to hope that having dangled a relative threat, so to speak, above the commandant's head, we might all find a semblance of continued safety.

CHAPTER 24

GOINGS AND COMINGS – APRIL 1942

As Jewish families continued to disappear from Verdun, orphaned children began appearing at la Clinique Meuse. Henri would arrive every few weeks with one or two of various ages. Other than the ever-present condition of hunger, there was only occasionally a significant physical concern, but always their countenance spoke of loss and fear.

"Bonjour, Nurse Marie. Today I am but passing through in the company of three new friends. Before they pay a visit to Rose and Bernard for a time, they have come to meet you."

The children stood close to Henri and each other as I knelt to make their acquaintance. "*Bonjour, tout le monde.* And who might you children be?" I asked, surveying their persons for any signs of physical distress and seeing none other than too-thin bodies and an emptiness in their eyes that spoke of much deeper concerns.

The children merely looked down, hesitant to speak and lost in their hurt.

"We are so very sorry that you are apart from your families. We will keep you safe until this hard time is over. Now, tell me your names so I may remember you when I see you next."

A boy of perhaps seven spoke up, holding tightly to the hand of the little girl next to him. "I am Luc, and this is my little sister, Élise. She is only five. She is very scared, but I am not."

Élise nodded her small head in agreement, her thumb never leaving her mouth. Their dark wavy hair and soulful brown eyes tore at my heart.

"I am glad to meet you both. You and Élise are very brave, and I can see you are taking good care of each other."

Turning to the third child, also a boy, I asked, "And you, young man, what is your name?

"Michel. I am Michel and I am eight years old. I have a sister, too, but I could not find her." Tears sprang from his hazel eyes as I gave him a gentle hug.

"Hopefully, Michel, your sister will be found soon. What is her name?"

"Camille. She is just four. But she is very brave, like Luc."

Luc leaned across Élise and said to his friend, "We will find her, Michel. Henri says he will look for her."

I turned to Henri, tears in my own eyes. "Have you and your new friends been to the convent for a meal? These young ones look as though some food and drink would be welcomed. And you, too, Henri. You look as though you have not eaten in days."

"Oui, oui, Nurse Marie. The good Sisters served us hearty soup and warm bread and packed two baskets of food that are safely stowed in my wagon and will be delivered to Rose along with the children."

Henri again used his wagon and my own Horse to cart and carry his illicit goods and cargo. His beloved Donkey had passed on many years ago, and I still missed throwing my arms round his thick, warm neck and holding tight to him. Horse, who was still young in spirit and sturdy of constitution despite his advanced years, served as a suitable replacement and seemed very pleased to have such a position of importance.

Henri's beautiful old peddler's wagon so better suited my image of who he was than that shiny thing of a vehicle that the commandant appropriated early into these two years of occupation. My dear friend made his way north and south along the same roads he traversed a lifetime ago—before this current war—selling, bartering, and buying, caring for those in our rural countryside and tending to each of us as only Henri could.

Now, once again, he was transporting goods, but goods of a different sort, the fragile human sort. Henri made sure he was seen several times a week rolling up and down the road between Verdun and south past my clinic and his home. The Germans had initially stopped him, often weekly, to search the insides of his wooden vehicle, but finding only worthless relics Henri ostensibly tried selling as valuable antiques to every German officer that demanded he open the wagon's tailgate, they began to leave "the crazy old peddler" to himself. Every few weeks, Henri now carried this most precious cargo, these young lost children, knowing that he could again be stopped at any time. To our benefit, as the war waged on and the Germans needed more men at their battlefronts, many soldiers left Verdun, and those that remained tended to stay in or close to the city, leaving us much freer to go about our business without harassment.

As was our custom when Henri brought children to the clinic, I gave them each a small honeyed sweet and sat them side by side atop my plinth table behind the tapestry screen. Henri then moved back to the locked door, keeping an eye to the window as I quickly took stock of the children.

After checking for head lice, conjunctivitis, and any other obvious physical concerns, aside from the fact that all three were undernourished they were well enough to travel on to Rose and Bernard's. "Henri, with so many frequent young guests, Rose and Bernard must be close to running out of room. How are the two of them managing with extra houseguests?"

"They are well and, yes, quite well out of room." I opened my mouth to speak but Henri shut his eyes and held up a hand toward me. "Do not ask the details, Marie. What you do not know keeps us all safer when the commandant comes to pry you for information. And yes, we need to discuss ideas to expand accommodations."

"I have told you countless times that I am ready to assist further and tired of waiting to be included in whatever schemes it is you hatch. I need to be part and parcel of these plans, Henri."

In response, a smile crossed his lips as he walked over to stand beside me. Taking my elbow in his hand, he said, "Oui, ma chère, now is the time, and let us speak this evening over a light supper, a last supper so to speak, in my home."

"Last supper? What is that about?"

"We will talk this evening when I return."

"Will Bernard be joining us?"

"No, just we two." He gave my cheeks a quick kiss and turned his attention to the children, who were now jumping off the table. I gave them all another sweet as they once again clung to Henri.

Before departing, Henri stopped in the doorway and turned. "Do you still have the linens in your Lavender House closets?"

"From the days of caring for the young soldiers? I haven't thought in years about what might still be upstairs, but unless they have been consumed by rodents or age, they should still be there."

"*Bien.* And until I return, you might think upon what else is in your house that could be useful in accommodating clandestine guests."

I gave each child a tight hug and watched them climb into the back of the wagon, Henri looking up and down the road before giving them a boost inside and closing the tailgate. He checked that the wagon's side slats were slightly open, providing air and a little light to his passengers, before mounting the driver's seat and urging Horse forward with a final wave.

I paused in the door's archway, wondering what sort of accommodations he would be asking of me. I was quite eager for his return. I had lingered long enough in this state of unrest, useless, an observer only, and was ready to provide greater assistance in any way whatsoever.

The remainder of the afternoon passed with nothing unusual occurring. A few people came complaining of sleeplessness and headaches, but who among us was not suffering from those same maladies—the classic symptoms of stress. I sent them away with sachets of lavender buds and small bags of chamomile tea.

Two young soldiers appeared about four in the afternoon, displaying identical rashes on their arms and shyly telling me they had runny bowels and stomach pain. They appeared more frightened than ill, and with some prodding

I understood they were extremely worried they had a "vulgar disease." I assured them they did not demonstrate symptoms of any venereal disease, but more likely they contracted their symptoms from unsanitary habits, such as not washing their hands frequently or eating foods already contaminated.

I had them thoroughly scrub their dirty hands and arms to their elbows using soap of lye and lavender made by the Sisters. While they were washing, I brewed a tea from blackberry leaves and put the strong concoction into tall glass jars they could take with them.

Applying ointment to their rashy arms, I instructed, "You need to consume large amounts of water as well as taking the blackberry tea. Dilute it one to one with water and drink a cup three times a day until the tea is gone. And tend better to your personal hygiene—wash after you use the toilet, before you eat, and keep your hands out of where they do not belong. If your symptoms have not subsided in three days, come to the clinic again."

With sheepish *mercis* after handing Sister payment, they left smelling quite nicely of blackberries and lavender. With their greatest fear eliminated, I did not think I would see them again.

Darkness had fallen when Henri finally pulled his wagon round the back of his home. Horse neighed loudly, letting me know he would appreciate his dinner. I grabbed a woolen shawl from the back of my desk chair, throwing it about my shoulders, and went to feed my horse and converse with my friend. Horse was already eating as Henri set about unhitching the wagon.

"Did you deliver your goods safely?"

"Indeed. The roads were quiet on this Saturday evening. The Germans are all in town celebrating another military victory of some kind."

As Horse finished his meal, I brushed his dark coat then sat down on a bale of hay, leaning my back against the shed wall, waiting patiently for Henri to begin. I knew little of his activities with the Resistance but did know he continued his involvement in the forging of documents and had for many years. The new papers were printed in Reims and given to Jews, allowing them to assume Gallic ancestry as they attempted to flee the country, many to Spain. I understood his protective nature in our relationship—he often told me my job was to heal, not to wage resistance, and I saw upon his face even now his internal struggle to include me in his plans. He knew full well I would agree to any activity that would help thwart the Nazis and save lives. I was fearless in that regard.

"Enough stoic silence, Henri. What is it you are plotting that will involve my assistance?"

He settled Horse into his stall, saying, "Shall we go inside and I'll prepare a meal?"

"No, my friend. You will join me here on this mound of hay and talk until you have told me everything."

He stood silently for several long seconds, just looking at me sitting atop the hay, before dropping down beside me with a thud. A great cloud of dust rose from the bale, and I quickly placed my shawl across my mouth and nose but kept my eyes fastened to Henri's face.

"More and more children are abandoned as their parents are rounded up and sent away. In a last desperate attempt to save them, the parents sometimes leave the children with neighbors, friends, and acquaintances—or give them to anyone in the moment of chaos before the parents are taken. Some older and able children flee as their parents tell them to run and not look back. They are found later along the back roads, in fields, or wandering lost in the streets of town after dark.

"Good souls like Bernard and Rose often take them in and, for a little while at least, they are made safe and comfortable. But often the very ones who rescue the young are frightened themselves, fearing they and theirs will be sent off next if a Jewish child is found among them. They come asking what to do. They seek help from Father Aubrey, Father O'Hara, Sister Évangéline, anyone they think might know of a place for the children until the war is over. We need to find a way to keep these innocents who come to us safe, to keep them from being stolen away to the camps to die along with their parents. We know from firsthand accounts that these are not just work camps for Jews and others deemed unworthy. There are substantiated rumors of death camps where people are being slaughtered by the Nazis."

At the mention of slaughter, I thought of Tanvir and my heart gave a great heave of grief. I forced my mind to steel itself and take charge of my emotions. Looking directly into Henri's clear eyes, I balled my fingers into tight fists, tears held back by the bite of nails pressed painfully into the palms of my hands.

"We must find a way to save the ones we can, Marie. I can secure the documents, but I cannot alone secure places for them to live."

"And my empty house. All those rooms waiting for them! Oui, oui! Mais oui!"

"The Germans appear to be looking the other way since the Catholic church began operating or expanding orphanages already on their property. There are many convents across France and Belgium taking children in.

"There is certainly no room at our small convent for any more bodies, and other than Hélène, the Sisters are too aged to educate and tend young children. Since the Germans already assume you and your clinic are an extension of the Catholic church and the convent, perhaps there is opportunity here as well."

"Do you mean opportunity to help other than using my house to hide the children?"

"I do. The little ones are too young to live unsupervised, too small to make the trek to Spain or safe houses where the Resistance workers are taking some of the older ones. I have been thinking, Marie. I am seldom home, here, next to your clinic with the walls between us still. I find it easier to spend my nights at my shop in Verdun or on the road. In town I can observe what is happening, and that is where my own contacts are located."

Sensing words I was not prepared to hear, I forced my hands to relax and leaned against Henri's shoulder. "What are you saying, my friend?"

Henri stood and began pacing the small area in front of the stacked hay. "I have given up on you ever agreeing to marry me. But are we not good together, the two of us? A strong team that can accomplish much, yes? Could we not, together, have my house become the convent's orphanage school for the older ones, with legal papers attesting to their non-Jewish patronage, while your house becomes a place for the youngest to live in hiding until they can enter the convent school or homes are found elsewhere?"

Henri not living next to me? Not here beside me? It was certainly true he was seldom home, true that the Germans had confiscated all the beautiful furnishings in his house, leaving him only a battered old table, one rickety chair, and a mattress upon his floor. But I had become accustomed to the sense of security knowing his home was so close, he was so close, even if away, and now my already broken heart wrenched again at the thought of his leaving. Another one I loved abandoning me.

A pain of selfish guilt caught in my throat at the truth of his words. I would, indeed, never become his wife, nor anyone's. I would never live with Henri in his home next to my clinic. It was space that needed filling, and what better use of his empty home than to become a school for these abandoned children who literally had nothing. And Henri was offering me the opportunity I had wanted: the opportunity to help in a meaningful way.

Standing up quickly from the hay, I said the only words I could: "I'm hungry, Henri. Let's go in and eat at your table. I will bring one of my chairs and pencils and paper. Tonight we will make plans for both the convent school and to keep the littlest ones safe in my house. We will make lists of all that is needed. Bernard and Rose will be grateful and relieved to have fewer in their own home, and I know they will help us with the younger ones, especially Rose."

We sat in his dining room at the small, wobbly table, left in place of the fine, solid, polished one taken by the Germans, both of us thinking it was, perhaps, as Henri had said, our last time alone in what had been such a sanctuary of beauty and peace. I thought of Félix here as a young boy, the three of us eating our evening meals together each day, helping Félix with his schoolwork, reading him stories, and tucking him into bed before I walked the short distance to the convent and my own empty bed.

Hours passed, with me returning several times to the clinic to retrieve more paper and sharpen our pencils. Henri and I plotted and planned, making list after list and drawing out how we would reconfigure this space in which we sat into a small school and my Lavender House into a safe sanctuary. I was feeling more alive than in all the past two years. Finally, at last, I would be doing something to help!

"You know, Henri, the commandant is literally frightened to death to even ride past my bee-infested property. He knows my home is empty, and I do not think it holds any interest to him. This certainly helps ensure the children hiding there will do so relatively safely."

"Actually, your house has not been entirely empty." He dropped his head, running his hands through his hair, letting me know that he was about to share with me news that I would find difficult. "Several times during this last month there have been too many children to stay with Rose and Bernard. Some of them have occasionally had to stay in your house with Rose."

My giddiness evaporated, instantly replaced by anger. "You have allowed people to stay in my home? How dare you take anyone into my house without my knowing!"

"Yes, yes, Marie. It has caused me many sleepless nights. Involving you was the last thing I intended, but there was absolutely no place for the children to go. I realized that your home is strategic—lies close by Rose and Bernard's, is anathema to the commandant because of your bees, and could truly suffice as a real home for these traumatized children. Telling you sooner would have been better than telling you after the fact, I realize that now, but I kept thinking I could find another way, another way to keep you safe as well as the children."

It was my turn to hang my head and pause long before I spoke. My heart was pounding in frustration, but I also understood Henri's overriding need to always protect me. "You know I love and respect you, Henri, and have always felt we could trust each other. Which is why I do not take lightly your acts of duplicity that, in your mind, are acts that keep me 'safe.' I have never appreciated that attitude, your lying by omission to shield me, and certainly do not now."

I clenched my teeth and took a slow breath to ease my frustration. "Over these many years, together we have overcome a great many odds. You say it yourself, we are a good team. So why, oh why, would you withhold this from me, your trespassing into my home? To risk ourselves is nothing; to risk the children is everything. It is my home, Henri, mine to determine what happens within its walls. It was never for you to determine otherwise."

"Oui, oui. Of course you are right to be angry with me." Henri reached across the battered old table and took my hands into his. "I love you, Marie. Forgive me for not allowing you to be strong enough on your own. It is hard for me to place you in what might become a tenuous situation after all you have suffered. I see the heartache you still carry, and I am, again, so sorry for the loss of your dear friend Tanvir. I do not want you to suffer additional trauma or be placed in harm's way because of any scheme I concoct."

He looked away with a heavy sigh before meeting my eyes again. "I know you were in love with Tanvir. You asked before if I was jealous of your love for him. I had to constantly remind myself that the capacity of the heart to love many was a gift and not a curse. And now, with this opportunity to aid these lost children, perhaps by helping them we can help heal ourselves."

"I love you too, Henri. But I love you most when you treat me as an equal, trusting that together, without deception, we can accomplish much. By saving these children from the wrath of war, we may indeed save ourselves as well. Trust and hope, Henri, trust and hope."

My lingering frustration gradually evaporated into further understanding, and at midnight, Henri rose one last time to fill our wine glasses as I replaced the guttering candles. We still had much to complete. It was past three in the morning, our plans constructed, when we retired onto Henri's mattress, falling into exhausted sleep, holding the future of many, including one another's, in our joined hands.

CHAPTER 25

THE HIDING HOUSE – MAY 1942

The four of us—Bernard, Rose, Henri, and myself—met in my home shortly after my conversation with Henri, laying out the plans we had conjured late into the night for both the convent school and my Lavender House. Rose was fully committed to caring for the young children and, since she had already been doing so in my home, had prepared lists of her own as to what would be needed. We compared notes and forged a master list of items to be secured to make the house adequate for the little ones.

"I must say, I have felt like such a traitor, Marie, but Henri made me promise not to say a thing until we knew if using your home was even a workable option."

Glancing at Henri, a feigned look of frustration on my face, I put my hand on Rose's. "No need for apologies. We are all of the same mind, and I do believe this plan will work. But we must be cautious and careful. We are fortunate that so many soldiers have left and those that remain seem to have no interest or time to worry about an empty house far from Verdun. Although the commandant will likely not set foot on my property, he could at any time send his men round again."

And so, over a period of three weeks, we quietly and gradually accumulated our stockpile. We could not purchase clothes for them or buy fabric—both of which were scarce, at any rate, and such purchases could arouse suspicion—so Henri asked for donations from the surrounding families. He did this frequently anyway, as the church always gathered items for those in need. And our friends and neighbors were generous with what little they had. Canned foods, used clothes, soap, odd lengths of fabric, toiletries, blankets, sheets, and towels were donated. Some were more than a bit worn, but we were extremely grateful. I already had a kitchen with enough pots, pans, dishes, cups, and utensils for however many mouths we had to feed.

"How many children are currently with you and Bernard?" I asked Rose.

"Four, at present. Henri has brought us ten over the last two months."

"I found what I believe to be permanent homes for six of them, and they are now with families as far away as Reims. But there are more and more children of all ages being abandoned, and I expect there will shortly be an even greater need," Henri said.

"I think the house could accommodate six total. Do you think you could care for and supervise that many?"

"I do," said Rose. "And although I have not asked, I think Bernard's daughter, Philippa, could be someone to stay here and help as well. She is living with Félicité and Eugénie, and when we visit her there for dinner, and she and I have a few minutes alone, she tells me she is extremely bored and needs to find employment. She does not know about the children, but I think she would be willing to get involved. She is strong in her sentiments regarding the Germans, and I also find her a woman to be trusted. She is intelligent, and I believe she would be empathetic and enthusiastic in helping us."

I then turned to Bernard, who had been silent for some time. "What do you think, Bernard? I understand that things between you and Philippa have not always been cordial. How do you find your daughter now that she has returned?"

"Well, when we are all together for dinner at my sister's, I don't really have anything to say. Philippa and Rose hit it right off and gab on with Eugénie and Félicité, and I just eat and barely listen. She hasn't really been here long enough for me to get reacquainted. She was but a small thing when she left with her mother, so she really is a stranger. I have nothing against her helping, but how would this work with Eugénie? I think she is hoping Philippa becomes their full-time housekeeper and caregiver."

"Philippa is still a young woman, and I would think she'd want to do something more interesting than devote all her time to catering to two elderly women who are still healthy and happily independent," Henri said.

"I think it's worth asking her. If she is interested, she could live here and perhaps we could pay her," I said. "I know I could give her a monthly stipend—not much, but perhaps enough that she would welcome a place where she was in charge of her days. But, as Henri says, what would Félicité and Eugénie need to be told?"

Henri ran his fingers through his hair, showing a little more salt than pepper these days, seriously considering the ramifications of bringing Philippa into the scheme. "We know you will need help, Rose, managing six children and the animals at Marie's as well keeping up your own place. If you agree, Bernard—and you too, Rose—and think Philippa would be trustworthy and amenable to the proposal, I think Rose should talk with her. If she is interested, we can have her come meet with us here and then go from there.

"She will need to do this without letting on to her aunt that a change may be coming. Félicité and Eugénie, while kind and generous women, are also fond of gossip and intrigue. It is very important we keep the plans for Lavender House between as few people as possible. Bernard and I will come up with a plausible explanation as to why Philippa will not be with them every hour of every day. Perhaps in the beginning, and to see if it works for everyone, Philippa can be here with Rose a few days a week and spend the weekends with her aunt and Félicité."

That next week found Philippa sitting with us round my table at Lavender House, ready to help with the children. She emanated a dynamic energy that suited her broad girth and tall stature. She was my height, at least. Her olive skin, auburn hair, and brown eyes mirrored Bernard's own. But her countenance was full of life and brighter than her papa's; she was quick to smile and equally quick with a witty retort or comment.

Philippa also demonstrated keen insight into what was needed and how the shared duties of caring for the children could be accomplished. It was obvious she and Rose had gotten to know each other well in the short time she had been here; they enjoyed each other's company, thought similarly, and I was reassured that they would work well together.

"I have told Tante Eugénie and Félicité that I want to spend more time with Papa and Rose—that Papa is going to teach me the business of raising sheep. Since they want nothing to do with smelly animals or coarse farming but are happy with my wanting to spend time with Papa, they were immediately agreeable and even offered to let me drive their automobile when I told them I would be staying two to three nights a week at the farm. But I assured them that Papa would pick me up and bring me back. I do not think we want evidence of any vehicle at Lavender House and especially one not usually seen there."

"Good thinking, Philippa! And just so you know, daughter, my sheep are never smelly. And I do think it an excellent idea that you learn all I can teach you about sheep ranching."

"Perhaps, Papa, you smell much like your sheep and therefore no longer notice their pungent aroma?"

Bernard chuckled and was obviously extremely happy to have this engaging young woman part of his family again. We were all glad to have her with us and grateful that, on her own, she had come up with a plausible explanation to share with her aunt.

We all agreed Lavender House must always appear empty, and therefore, it was imperative that the animals be kept as hidden as the children. And any of us coming or going from Lavender House would leave our horses, wagons, or autos at Bernard and Rose's home and then walk to and from the house, entering and leaving only by the kitchen door. In winter, this would ensure no tracks would appear in the snow leading from the road up to the house. All would appear uninhabited.

I had taken to spending my Sundays at Lavender House instead of the convent. I would leave the clinic at dusk on Saturday and return at sunrise on Monday. That one full day allowed me to be a part of all the activity and goings on—taking stock of the children and animals, discussing things with Rose and

Philippa, and observing how they were all faring. Henri would often be there as well, and we would sleep on army cots in my sitting room, among the caged chickens and rabbits now sharing permanent residence with the children.

The cages were lined up in two rows across the east wall of my sitting room, with our cots set up at night in the area between them and the dining room. Waking in the early morning to the sounds of hungry animals scratching and cackling for their breakfast paired with the raucous noise of little ones running across the floorboards overhead was astounding. This house of mine, now full of unknown tomorrows, was full of vivid life in the present. Even with the worry and uncertainty of our future, these were the happiest days of my week, perhaps of my life, when I felt renewed with a restoration of purpose and courage. Where I gathered my hope for the week ahead.

The Sisters and I decided that if anyone inquired as to my whereabouts on Sundays, they were to be told I was in my room next to the chapel, where I was resting, praying, and meditating and was under no circumstances to be disturbed. I did not think much about what dismay this falsity caused the Sisters until one Sunday morning when I was truly in my bed at the convent, a chest cold having overtaken me. I would be going nowhere for a few days.

Early that morning, heavy rain pounding on our roof, I was lying awake and coughing loudly when I heard loud pounding on the convent's front door. The knocking was insistent, sending Sister Jeanne scurrying from the kitchen to answer. There stood Commandant Reichenbach and his usual cadre of two uniformed cronies, one on each side, their three faces hard as steel and their demeanors resolute.

"I need to see Nurse Durant immediately," demanded the commandant. "Go get her. Now."

"I have told you thrice Sundays before, Herr Kommandant, that she is not to be disturbed on this holy day. And this Sunday she lies in her bed sick with a terrible cold and coughing out her poor lungs."

Right on cue, I began to cough uncontrollably, truly sounding as though my lungs were about to be expelled from my body.

"Can you not hear the poor thing? And besides, she is surely contagious—most likely becoming sick from all your men coming to the clinic with these same symptoms," accused Sister Jeanne. "Between her usual patients and now all your ailing soldiers, our sister is exhausted."

The remaining nuns came to join Sister Jeanne in the foyer, all standing stoutly in the doorway before the Germans and barring them entrance into our convent.

"Sister Marie? So, she is indeed your Catholic Sister, part of this rickety convent?"

"What did you think, Commandant? Marie is our sister in every sense of the word. Now leave us. We have our own Sunday absolutions to attend to, as I suggest you do yourself. I do not doubt that you have much to atone for." With that, Sister Jeanne attempted to firmly close and bar the door. But the commandant was quick, pushed through, and nearly ran the short distance around the corner and past the chapel to my small alcove of a room, being led to my presence by the sounds of another severe coughing spell.

I heard his heavy footfalls, knew he was coming to confirm I was indeed here and in my bed.

"Hello, Commandant," I said hoarsely between coughs accompanied by colored phlegm, which I made sure he saw before covering it with the rag I spit into. He covered his mouth and nose, turned, and retreated as quickly as he had come.

The commandant never again attempted to disturb my Sundays but now appeared even more frequently at my clinic, as though to make up for allowing me my day of rest. That was both a relief and a worry. If he was not looking for me at the convent, where might he look next? Perhaps he did believe I remained in my room every Sunday, pious woman that I was.

Despite my worries regarding the commandant, we went on with our work. I had a sewing machine at the house, and between the blankets, linens, used clothing, and donated fragments of cloth, and what was long stored in my upstairs closet, Rose and I were often busy making repairs or alterations to the children's clothing.

The welcome light lingered with the long summer days, and late Sunday evenings found me still sewing. Henri, in his ever-convincing way, continued to gather donations from all the families he visited—we put to use virtually anything he obtained. Each child, regardless of age, was given two sets of clothes when they first came to Lavender House, in addition to a new name and papers attesting to their Christian and French identity. Any yellow stars we found on their existing garments we cut into tiny pieces, Bernard burning them in his iron barrel at his farm.

CHAPTER 26

HIDDEN TREASURE 1942

As soon as the children were brought into the house and Henri secured their new identities, they were from then on called only by their new names, all very French, safe, and gentile. We attempted to keep them as close as possible to their given names. We loved them equally, and the children soon became close to one another, a bonded and protective family.

The little ones in Lavender House were unknown to all, hidden in what we hoped and trusted was a cloak of safety. Those age two to six lived there under Rose and Philippa's day-to-day care. When old enough for school, they would transition to living in the convent school, as room became available. The plan was that, when possible, the older children would make their way to safety either by becoming a son or daughter to families in the area or when Bernard, Henri, and brave others found for them transport to safer places. A few, with the help of guides in the Resistance, made the trek to Switzerland and some on to Spain. There were at any given time, from 1942 through 1944, ten children in the convent school and seven to nine young ones in my house.

Now that we had to feed the hidden children, who had no ration cards, we needed a garden larger than the convent's and my small plots outside the back door. In the spring, under the cover of darkness, Bernard and Henri cleared a sizable area of ground at the edge of dense lavender near the back of the fields just a short distance from Rose's house. The ever-growing mound of chicken manure (which was moved under cover of night as well) provided adequate fertilizer, and our variety of vegetables grew well. The garden was partially hidden by an ancient, towering oak tree that I often found myself meandering toward when needing a moment of quiet contemplation. Its tall, wide, crisscrossed branches with clusters of broad green leaves did not obscure the afternoon's sunlight yet provided enough cover to make the garden difficult to see from passing vehicles and hopefully from any planes flying overhead.

As food became ever more scarce, the Germans began confiscating more and more from the rural farms. There was often no food to be given to those with valid ration cards—the bakeries had no flour to make bread, there was no meat and few vegetables or fruits. People took to fishing the Meuse regularly and drying or canning their catches. Most of those who had been farmers were now German laborers, and the land where crops once grew lay untended and fallow. There was little feed for livestock, much less for the people of France. We continually squirreled our food away in crevices, much as we tucked our hidden children into the corners of the hiding house.

We knew we were fortunate to grow what we needed to survive and shared as we could the excess of our hidden garden with our neighbors. We also knew that at any moment the Germans could raid my home and property, sending all of us, including the children, to the work camps. As the war raged on, we heard more bone-chilling rumors of death camps in Germany, Austria, and Poland. Henri told us of firsthand reports of such places coming from civilians, escapees, and those working with the French Resistance. The horror of it was beyond my understanding. The absolute horror of the reality of what humans could inflict upon their own was beyond belief. And yet, on and on it went. Henri and Bernard continued their clandestine work with the Resistance, and while they never shared their secrets, I lived knowing they risked their lives to keep so many safe.

Between my constant concern for Henri and Bernard, the continual surreptitious intrusions from the commandant, my responsibilities in the clinic, and overseeing the welfare of the children, I had more than enough consuming my own allotment of worry.

CHAPTER 27

THE CONVENT SCHOOL – NOVEMBER 1942

I do not know and did not ask where Henri came up with two pairs of knitting needles and three large bags filled with a variety of colored skeins of yarn. With these the Sisters knit mittens, hats, and sweaters of many colors to keep the children almost warm during the cold months of winter. At the house, we could use only kerosene heaters so there would be no tell-tale smoke rising from the chimneys. The smell, even with windows cracked, was foul and oily. Again, where Henri found the scarce fuel to keep the heaters lit, I did not know. We used it sparingly.

The vicious winter of 1942 proved unforgiving and harshly cold. Whether in the convent school beside the woodstove fire or at my home in front of the kerosene heaters, many nights the children huddled together in twos and threes, sleeping in makeshift communal beds for warmth.

It was bleak and spare of all we needed to live. News of the war was always that the Germans had succeeded in yet another invasion, another victory, and more people sent to the camps. We did not know the location of all the so-called work and detention camps nor the ultimate fate of those that were taken away. But as time passed, the unthinkable became the reality for millions of lost souls. America was still determined to stay out of the war, and the efforts of our own European allies, also under siege, seemed futile and ineffective, including those of the French Resistance.

Our primary goal became finding enough food and staying warm. We always seemed to find fabric scraps, some remnants from somewhere to patch us up and keep us covered, but we were perpetually cold and hungry. The children became thin, our spirits were empty, and our hearts were as hollow as our stomachs.

One such gloomy winter's day, the Germans arrived at my clinic door—the usual three, Commandant Reichenbach and his two stoic young officers, never a surprise after two years of his frequent "visits." This day, the commandant requested an inspection of the convent school and insisted I accompany him next door to make the introductions as he conducted his visit.

"And tell me, Nurse Durant, how many children are kept next to you and what are their ages? Do they just appear at your door, these French children?"

"Most of them are brought by relatives who have no place for them nor a way to feed and clothe another body. They are usually delivered to the cathedral in Verdun. Father Aubrey takes them in, and if we have the room, the good Father brings them on to our school. The school can house and teach twelve children who are at least six years of age and usually no older than twelve. The older children help with the younger. The Sisters cook their meals, repair their clothing, and help the children attend to their personal hygiene and spiritual life. Here, they are cared for and cared about. It would be best if they had their parents and actual homes, but their families were torn apart by this war. We do the best we can for them, as is our duty in the sight of God."

Putting on my best Catholic mantle, I continued, "Sister Hélène instructs them both academically and spiritually, providing as sufficient a Catholic education as the times and circumstances allow. We feel it our Christian duty to take these children and care for them. They have nothing to sustain them besides the compassion of the Church. Many of their fathers were conscripted for work in Germany and the mothers sent to work elsewhere in factories. Basically, these French children are made orphans by the war."

After Félix left for America, Hélène spent more and more of her time at the convent with the Sisters. In their midst she found contentment, and in their faith, found her spiritual home. The Sisters welcomed her into their fold and, along with Father Aubrey, taught her the ways of a nun. She took her vows in the cathedral in Verdun in the late summer of 1941, becoming the youngest Sister in our convent. Having already attended university, when approached with the idea of becoming the teacher to the convent's new school, she eagerly embraced the opportunity. The children loved her, and she protected this young flock of hers as a mother would. We were extremely thankful for her skills and her compassionate dedication to the children.

My lengthy description completed, I walked with the commandant through the clinic and knocked upon the school's door. It was quickly opened by Sister Hélène, her fingers at her lips, indicating we were to enter quietly.

"The children are all taking their early sleep, and this is not a good time for visitors."

Despite Sister's directive words, the commandant stepped hastily across the doorway, asking, "Why are they all asleep? It is only just past noon."

"After their meager lunch, the children are tired. They are always tired and always hungry. I teach for short intervals and then we rest. It is difficult for these young students to listen to the words of their teacher over the demanding sounds of their stomachs. The Sisters have very little from which to make them meals with any sustenance. We do the best we can. And what did you have for your dinner last evening, Herr Kommandant?"

"Do not be insolent with me, girl. It is not your place."

"I am not a girl. I am a nun. I am Sister Hélène, and my place is here with these lost ones. I am doing the work of our Lord. And whose work are you doing, Commandant?"

They locked eyes with one another for long tension-filled seconds, neither one glancing away, neither one capitulating nor acquiescing to the other. One of the younger children began to cry softly, allowing me the opportunity to intercede between these two agitated people.

"We will let you get back to tending your wards, Sister. Thank you for taking the time to show the commandant our school." With that, I began to walk back through the clinic door, hoping the commandant would follow suit, which he did not.

Instead, he walked the perimeter of the schoolhouse, opening and peering into every closed cabinet and drawer. I held my breath as he approached the closet where I hid medical supplies I knew could be taken by the Germans. I prepared for that happening now, that my precious, rare supplies would be confiscated, all that were left of the last shipment to arrive from Félix and Solange before the occupation. But the closet held only school supplies used by the children. The commandant rummaged through an array of pencil stubs, short pieces of white chalk, small chipped black slate boards, erasers, wooden rulers, and donated reading books used in the children's lessons but nothing else. Henri must have anticipated this eventuality and recently moved my cache. Bless you, Henri.

The commandant shut the closet door and stepped closer to where the children were lying upon their blankets, huddled together for warmth round the small woodstove in the center of the room. He stopped next to every sleeping child, lingering, examining closely their thin, pale faces.

From the floor where the children slept came a young voice tinged with awe yet filled with pleading. "Bonjour, Monsieur, your boots are very nice and very shiny. My name is Michel and I am eight years old. I am wondering if you might have seen my sister. Her name is Camille and she is only four. Have you come to give us some food? We could also use some wood. Do you have wood? We are awfully cold."

I saw on the commandant's face a fleeting acknowledgment of what these young ones were enduring, the sad state of their small, spare bodies and the longing they must feel for their parents. I stood amazed in that brief moment— the commandant standing stock still, feeling, perhaps, a semblance of humanity. Quickly wiping his hand across his face, as if removing all human emotion, the commandant turned and, without looking at me or Sister Hélène, walked through the school directly to its front door and outside to his waiting driver. He did not say a word to either of us as he departed, and for that I was grateful.

"Although I may have overstepped my bounds, I am not sorry I challenged that odious man. I don't know how you put up with his constant visits to the clinic. Hopefully he will not visit the school again, as I cannot promise I will not physically attack the beast."

"You did well, Sister. This may be the first time he truly looked into the faces of despair and saw the reality of deprivation. I do not think you will be bothered a second time."

I returned to the clinic, thinking it best to leave Sister Hélène alone to calm herself and focus on the children. My day went on as usual, tending to many patients with their constant worries and various ailments. Throughout the afternoon, I was happily distracted by the sounds of the children on the other side of the wall. How I relished their young voices singing, their frequent laughter, and, as always, hope won the day.

As the sunlight faded to dusk, I found myself thinking something must be done to find the children more food, and intended to talk with Sister Évangéline and Henri about bolstering our larder. We sorely needed a milking cow or even a couple of goats. If only those animals did not make noise. And there was no possible way to keep cows and goats in the house. What squawking there was between the children and the chickens was already worrisome.

The following day, and every week of the remaining freezing winter months, two boxes of foodstuffs, often milk, cheese, bread, and occasionally some meat, appeared outside the clinic door. I never knew what variety of foods would be found but was always beyond grateful. On several occasions, short stacks of wood would be left, which I immediately took to Sister Hélène for their fire. No note, no message ever accompanied these offerings, but I knew the commandant placed the provisions there. He not only heard Sister Hélène's words, but I imagined he saw in the haunted faces of the children, come to life in the innocence of Michel's pleas, their cold hunger and heavy hearts. I never made mention of these deliveries to anyone, not to a soul, and certainly not to the proud commandant. I found I had secrets of my own to keep.

CHAPTER 28

THE SUSTENANCE OF HOPE – DECEMBER 1942

The winter was proving more frigid than the Germans. The availability of food for day-to-day survival was meager, and even imagining anything special for the holidays was out of the question.

I told everyone that we would celebrate with the children in the convent school on Friday, the eighteenth, and at Lavender House on Saturday—midway between Hanukkah and Christmas. Since early November, the Sisters had been happily baking and crafting small gifts for all the children from provisions long hoarded. I asked the Sisters to please not make gifts that were in any way religious—neither Jewish nor Christian—as all were valiantly attempting to cope with their heart-wrenching separation. Especially at the convent school with the older ones, we made no mention of religion unless the children found comfort in what memories they brought with them, and those we secretly acknowledged.

The children in Lavender House were so young and traumatized that few could recount any memories other than their continued lament for their missing mothers. After a while, they seemed to relinquish even those memories, and all the children, youngest to oldest, seemed to live in a semblance of contentment with the others and those of us caring for them.

This December found twelve children in the convent school and ten hidden in my house; a full house on all accounts. Between Rose, Hélène, Philippa,

Bernard, Henri, myself, and the Sisters, we tenaciously held twenty-two young lives in our hands.

The Sisters delivered their presents to each child at the school while I took the nuns' gifts to Lavender House. The handmade gifts, thoughtfully crafted for each child, their names elegantly written on a tag, were wrapped in whatever paper was at hand and tied with twine. My offering to the children was macarons.

I had lamented to Henri some weeks earlier how wonderful it would be to taste macarons this holiday, wishing aloud that I might bake them for our children. Several years ago, Solange sent me our old cook's recipe for the most wonderful macarons, the ones we made with her every holiday of our childhood in Marseille. Until now, I'd felt no inkling to bake these memories of mine, but this year, we had so many children and almost nothing to offer them but hope. Henri made no comment to my wishful thinking, merely smiling and nodding his head. I thought nothing more about the possibility of such treats.

Henri being Henri, he once again worked his magic. One week before Christmas, he appeared in the convent kitchen with a box containing a small sack of flour, another of sugar, a short bottle of fragrant vanilla, and a ball of pale yellow butter. My own Père Noël come to make a miracle!

"Henri, let's bake the macarons together, here. It will be such a surprise! They will be our combined gift to the children."

"As you wish, ma chère, and we will have dinner together as well. I will ask the Sisters to please allow us sacred baking time—the two of us alone with their oven." He scooped the priceless ingredients back into the box, and with a sudden (and very surprising) lingering kiss to my cheek, he left the convent, calling behind him, "Dinner will be served at seven tomorrow. I will cook and then we will bake."

I felt a stir of happiness, a spark of the holiday made possible by Henri's excitement over our plan for tomorrow's time together. My dearest friend always making the best of a situation and finding a way to instill a sense of joy, even in such dire circumstances.

The next afternoon, after the clinic's closing at five, I completed my paperwork and hurried to the convent. It was approaching six o'clock when I came through the kitchen door to find Henri alone, tending to his cooking. Candles were lit round the room and the aroma of our meal emanated through the doorway.

"And where are the Sisters, Monsieur? Have you hidden them away?"

"They had already planned to spend the afternoon and evening with Father Aubrey, decorating the Verdun sanctuary for Christmas. He invited them to stay on for dinner. They most likely will not return before nine or so, quite an exciting evening for them as well."

"And one I am sure you and the good father planned in advance."

Henri feigned being affronted. "They always help decorate the cathedral. . . . But this year I did encourage Father to have them stay for a meal. I provided what ingredients they would need, and I am sure our good Sisters have commandeered the kitchen and planted Father Aubrey, along with Father O'Hara, firmly down before a blazing fire to observe their activities over fine cups of tea."

As Henri tended to our dinner, I set our table. "Do you remember our Christmas Eve here in '22? Bernard and the lambs and all the food the Sisters prepared?"

"Indeed I do. It was a fine evening. Such a snowstorm I braved that night! But what I remember most are those beautiful beeswax pillars you and the Sisters made that stood sentry around the edges of the room, their light reflecting your own luminescence."

"Oh, Henri," I laughed, "your impressions of me have always been generous. And now here we are again, twenty years on."

"Oui, and I still see your light, always your light of hope. It is my touchstone, your belief that all will be well in the end."

"And Henri, what do you believe?"

"I believe in survival, Marie."

"And hope. I know you believe in hope. You must."

"I will believe because you do, ma chère." He smiled and stood in front of me, taking my hands into his own. We stood there for many moments exchanging reminiscences, grateful that we were still here, together in Meuse.

That evening we dined on the contents of one of our jars of canned meat combined with preserved mixed vegetables, a finely chopped onion, and dried beans and spices from which Henri had concocted a rich cassoulet. He set the steaming pot on the table along with a half-bottle of burgundy, a good portion of which had already been added to the cooking pot.

I lit a thick beeswax pillar and placed it in the center of the kitchen table, its warm light glowing softly between us as we sat and ate our holiday meal. Letting the oven heat before commencing our baking, we ate slowly, lingering over the candlelight and conversation. We both agreed the food was never better, the most important ingredient being a generous portion of shared memories and tenacious hope.

CHAPTER 29

THE GATHERING – MAY 1943

As the brutal winter came to an end and spring slowly emerged, a discouraging thought presented itself to my mind. If the commandant was stung once again by my bees, or any bees for that matter, it was logical to surmise, based on his history of overt reaction, that life-threatening anaphylaxis was indeed probable. If any of my patients were at such high risk, I knew I would take measures to ensure I had an appropriate treatment prepared ahead of any medical emergency.

In my Pharmacologie classes at l'Hôpital de la Pitié-Salpêtrière, we had discussed the preparation of many dilutions, including *Apis mellifica*, which is prepared from the whole body of the honeybee. Dilution of *Apis mellifica* was often effective in treating reactions to insect stings, such as swelling and possible anaphylaxis. The bees were out in my fields this spring, and collecting the amount needed to concoct the dilution would be an easy enough chore. I did feel regret at having to sacrifice the lives of so many industrious, unsuspecting bees for the good of someone so abhorrent. However, as a nurse, there was little choice but to prepare the *Apis mellifica*, a process I had not previously attempted on my own but was eager to try.

Taking down my translated copy of Hahnemann's *Organon of Medicine*, I began reviewing my knowledge of homeopathic intervention. Samuel Hahnemann published his first writings on the subject of homeopathic dilutions in 1810 and was still considered the father of homeopathic medicine. Homeopathy was based on the Law of Similars, the premise being that every substance causing certain symptoms can also be used to treat and cure those symptoms using diluted doses of natural substances.

Epinephrine was most often used to treat anaphylaxis, but wartime shortages ensured there was no means of acquiring that medication. And because I preferred a natural plant-based treatment whenever possible, making the *Apis mellifica* myself was my preference and the only option available.

It was the time of year when bees tended to swarm, taking a queen with them and traveling sometimes just a short distance to begin a new, less-crowded hive. Although Bernard still kept his beloved sheep, barn, and ramshackle house, he and Rose chose to live in her small home at the far edge of my property, out beyond the large old tree under which the gardens grew. They had line of sight to Lavender House and the expansive fields, enabling them to observe much that went on around my home.

I now asked Rose and Bernard to keep an eye out for a swarm. Collecting from a swarm would be the easiest means by which to gather the bees I needed, as well as to start another thriving hive. Sister Hélène wanted to learn the ways of apiary and collecting was a good place to begin. It would also provide an opportunity for mother and daughter to spend time together. Since Rose's marriage to Bernard, her relationship with Hélène was strained. Rose, I knew, felt saddened that her daughter was so aloof and distant. Sister Hélène had not been able to come to terms with her mother "replacing" her father with someone she disliked as much as Bernard.

Bernard stopped by the clinic a week later to tell me he had spotted a swarm of honeybees clustered on a low branch of the big tree by the gardens. A swarm only remains still for a short time before the bees decide on a new site for a hive. During this period of calm, the tight cluster of bees is relatively docile, making collecting and moving them mostly sting-free and quick.

Walking into the convent school, I asked Sister Hélène if she could possibly leave for a short time and come with me to collect bees.

"I am so excited that you want me to help with a bee gathering. The timing is ideal, as the children are occupied with arithmetic lessons with Sister Marguerite."

Her students were indeed seated quietly round their study tables, chalk to slate as Sister Marguerite moved from one to another, checking and encouraging their efforts. Sister Hélène conferred with Sister Marguerite to let her know we would be gone the remainder of the afternoon, and we departed in my wagon. I knew Rose and Philippa would be at my house with the children, and we could collect Rose when we got there.

"I'm nervous, Marie. What if the bees decide to attack us?" Hélène asked as we climbed onto the wagon.

"That is unlikely to happen while they are congregated into a tightly packed cluster. Some of the bees take off to scout for a new residence while the majority stay behind, secured around their queen who is cloistered in the middle. If we get there soon and they are still quiet, it will not take long to gather what I need for my dilution and move the remainder into the clean hive I've brought. And, you will be wearing protective clothing, so there is really nothing to worry about."

In the back of the wagon, my basket contained extra clothing along with white protective garments and a large glass jar with a red metal lid to collect a good number of bees. I also had a clean Langstroth hive with only five frames (rather than the usual ten) and one frame was smeared with tempting honey. A short ladder, a large metal bucket, my saw, the wide-mouthed glass jar and lid, and a bottle of sugar-water to splash about the clean hive comprised my array of supplies. The presence of the sugar-water would keep the bees' attention once I moved them into their new home and would, hopefully, help them settle. It was imperative to assure the queen was moved as well. After all, their purpose was to protect and nurture their queen, and if she was present in the new home, then most likely all would transition nicely.

As we approached Rose's house, I said, "We need the help of your mother too. When we get to her house, jump down, hurry to Lavender House, tell her what is happening and then walk with her to the big tree by the gardens. That is where the swarm will be." I did not tell Hélène that Bernard was the one who told me of the bees. I wanted her to willingly assist Rose and myself and not become agitated at the mention of her stepfather. We wanted nothing and no one, neither women nor bees, agitated on this reconnaissance endeavor.

Without comment, Hélène did as she was asked. Before I completed carrying all my equipment to the tree, both mother and daughter appeared.

Just as Bernard had described, the swarm of bees was on a fairly low branch. The cluster itself was relatively small, and if I cut the branch as close to the cluster as possible, it would fit well inside my bucket.

"Let's get our clothes and veils on first and then we can carry everything to the tree." I had on heavy trousers, a thick flannel shirt, and gloves and only needed the hat with the veil to protect my face and head. Rose would wear my white protective clothes and the extra hat.

"Is that all you're wearing, Marie?" asked Hélène. "I am putting everything on and maybe your clothes as well."

"I seldom get stung, and there is even less chance with a swarm."

We carried our equipment over and laid it on the ground just a few feet from the swarm. "Rose, will you please hold the ladder while I climb and scrape the bees into the jar? That won't take but a minute or so. Then Hélène, you take the jar from me, screw the lid on securely, and next, hand me the saw. I will cut off the branch with the remaining bees, and we can put it in the bucket before transferring them, with their queen, into the hive."

All proceeded accordingly, and soon I was standing on the third rung of the ladder with a short, wide, metal scraping tool in my right hand, attempting to move the bees from branch to jar. They were buzzing loudly, tightly intertwined with one another's bodies, causing long strings of bees to separate from the cluster, and I could feel the warmth from their vibrating mass. I filled my wide-mouth jar three-quarters full, secured the lid tightly, and handed it down to Hélène, taking the saw from her. Neither woman had spoken to one another, but this was to be expected, as we were all intensely focused on our task.

"If we move the ladder forward and place you facing the branch, Marie, you can grab hold above the bees and saw it clean."

I agreed with Rose and climbed down. Together we placed the ladder where I could easily saw the branch off and put it into the bucket.

"Hélène, once I start sawing, would you please hold up the bucket, and I will gently lay the bees and their branch inside."

"What if they start to fly and I panic and drop it?"

"Would you rather hold the ladder and I will take care of the bucket?"

"Oui, Maman, that would suit me much better. I certainly don't want to be the cause of a failed attempt, and I just don't know how I would react if I got stung."

Mother and daughter changed places as I decided on the best angle for my cut. The branch was not thick, only half the diameter of my fisted hand. The sharp teeth of the saw caught traction on the slippery bark as soon as I began to cut.

The bees remained relatively calm, at least at the first of my passes, but then became slightly agitated by the noise and the movement of their resting place, and some began to fly. They flew away from us without intent to sting; however, it was enough to cause Hélène to make noises I had once heard from a goat stuck in barbed wire.

"Marie, hurry, hurry!" she squealed. "I can't hold the ladder much longer!"

"Don't be foolish, Hélène. You can and you will. Do not let go of the ladder under any circumstances." The ground was uneven and without her to steady the ladder I could well lose my balance. And lose everything.

Rose quickly rescued Hélène, the bucket in one hand and the other steadying the ladder and her nervous daughter. Then Rose began to sing what sounded to my ears a lullaby. To my surprise, Hélène began to sing as well, and I found my saw moving forward and back in rhythm to the melody of their sweet song. In that moment, my heart was filled with happiness, a gentle reminder that together we can do all things.

Rose handed up the bucket as the branch began to crack, Hélène's hands now firmly on the ladder and the bees still calm and ready for a new home.

I climbed down, and we moved a short distance into the lavender fields to a tower of three existing hives. Placing the clean hive on the ground, I handed the women the sugar-water, instructing them to splash it about the interior. Their laughter moved as music on the air as they teasingly made to splash one another before we transferred the bees from the branch into their clean and sweet-smelling home.

"Hélène, I am going to use the same tool with which I collected the bees to move them gently off the branch and into the hive. You stand beside me as I begin and then, if the bees remain calm, I want you to take the branch from me and continue transferring the remainder of them into the hive."

Hélène stepped close beside me, eyes intent on my actions. The bees did remain calm, as did Hélène, and as I handed her the branch to complete the task, I saw a satisfied smile on her face just behind her veil. The air between us all was now placid with success.

"That was amazing, Marie! I want to help every time you collect bees, and I do want to begin helping in the convent's honey house."

"Wonderful! You can bring the children and we can have apiary lessons. And then a lunch of honey and cakes."

"You were very brave, my daughter. Collecting stinging insects is not a job for the faint of heart. I am very proud of you. You definitely have a future in apiary," said Rose, placing an affectionate arm about her daughter's shoulders as we walked back to the wagon.

Rose stopped beside the wagon and grinned at us. "I am famished! You two come back to Lavender House, and I will make us all lunch. The little ones would love a surprise visit from you both. And perhaps I could persuade you to help clean the animals' pens while I make our food. Lunch will taste much better once the smells of the chickens, rabbits, and goat are not so prominent!"

Having accomplished all we set out to do, including lunch, pen cleaning, and a very congenial time with these wonderful women and precious little children, Sister Hélène, myself, and the bees headed back to my waiting patients and her waiting students. I even forgot to complain about a goat being in my home.

CHAPTER 30

PREPARING THE CURE – MAY 1943

After seeing to the day's remaining patients, I was eager to prepare the tincture. Arranging all I needed atop my work counter, I began. After placing on my scale an empty jar like that which housed the bees, I subtracted the weight of the empty jar from the one filled with the insects. The directions called for a proportion of 80% strong alcohol and 20% bees in weight.

I measured the alcohol accordingly and poured it over the bees. I would leave them for a few hours, cleaning the day's instruments and completing patient paperwork before finishing my task at hand.

Just as the sun began to drop into the horizon, I returned to my bees. Their still bodies again made me feel sad that they were sacrificed for another living being's life. I took a moment to bless the bees and then transferred some of them, with a small amount of alcohol, into my large stone mortar. Using the pestle, I slowly and firmly crushed their bodies; a musky fragrance filled my senses, reminding me of the smell of the blooming fields round my house.

I repeated the crushing process twice more, filling the empty glass jar each time with the macerated bees and alcohol. The tincture would now sit two weeks in the convent's dark, cool cellar among the jars filled with fruits and vegetables.

When shaken, the mixture became pale amber in color and would become darker still as the active substances migrated from the tissue of the bees into the alcohol. Each day before leaving the convent to begin my day of caregiving,

I made my way down the creaky wooden stairs into the dim cellar to shake the mixture. The process of creating what would hopefully prove to be effective was very exciting. In truth, I hoped the medicine would never need to be used. But the nurse in me knew it must be prepared should the situation arise—and for whomever might need this curative gift.

The two weeks of shaking the tincture each morning passed quickly. I arrived at the clinic early on Saturday, when I was more assured of quiet, and gathered the items I would need to complete the preparation. Nine glass vials with rubber stoppers, squares of cheesecloth, a funnel, and another large jar with a screw lid stood ready on my work surface along the back wall by the sink.

I filtered the bee-alcohol solution by laying one of the thin cheesecloths across a funnel and slowly pouring the dark amber solution through the cloth from one glass jar to the other. Using a square of paper and a small amount of fish glue, I labeled the contents "*Apis mellifica Teinture*," with the date, "29 May 1943," and the alcoholic degree, "80 deg."

The next step was to determine what dilution of the tincture to prepare. Being concerned that too low a dilution would pose a risk in a person known to be sensitive to bee venom, I opted for a 9CH (*centésimale hahnemannienne*) dilution, which would be administered sublingually to the patient, if needed.

Gathering the clean glass vials, I lined them up, applying labels numbered one through nine. I placed one drop of the amber-colored tincture into the first vial and carefully added to that ninety-nine drops of strong alcohol. If I miscounted, I would need to begin again. After maintaining a steady hand and precise counting, I placed a stopper in the vial and labeled it "1CH." After shaking the liquid gently to ensure no leakage, I banged my closed fist, the vial safely secured in the palm of my hand, against the solid side of the *Organon* tome to a count of thirty. This firm thwack of the vial against a solid surface, referred to in homeopathy as "succussion," would activate the potency of the dilution.

I spent the next thirty minutes repeating the same exacting process, using each successive vial to create dilutions from 1CH through 9CH. Labeling them accordingly and lining them up in my apothecary cabinet, I considered myself prepared should any of my patients find themselves experiencing acute symptoms brought about by my well-intentioned bees. Were we not all attempting to protect what was ours in whatever ways we could? Once more, I thanked my bees and got on about my day, protecting my patients regardless of who they were by whatever means I had available.

CHAPTER 31

A STINGING DILEMMA –
JULY 1943

The late afternoon sun streamed warmth through the window beside my desk and lulled me to drowsiness. Sister Dominique had already returned to the convent, allowing me time alone to catch up on my paperwork. But in my somnambulant state, I found I was having a difficult time keeping my eyes open. I had attempted to read the same first sentence of a journal article three times. This was just before my clinic door exploded open by two familiar soldiers, heavily supporting the body of their half-bent-over superior.

I came to attention at once. The commandant was obviously in severe distress and obviously from bees, most likely mine—yet again! At my direction, the young men laid him prone on my examining table and continued to hover at my heels, terror in their eyes. They knew, as I was sure their commander did, that this current episode of stings held the possibility of fatal consequences.

Elevating his head and shoulders did not ease his labored breathing. Flushed of face and neck with acute general swelling, hives had begun to appear along his torso, arms, neck, and face. He struggled against us as we undressed him down to his shorts, where barbs were still encased in swollen welts.

"*Erbrechen*," he whispered.

"What is he saying?"

"That he is going to vomit, '*erbrechen*,'" one of the young men replied.

"Hand me the bowl from the back shelf," I said, pointing.

I took the bowl and said to the commandant, "Go ahead and be sick if you need to, but you also must try and calm yourself, Friedrich. You know how important it is to focus on your breathing and not panic.

"This time, as I am sure you are feeling, is more serious than when you were last here from stings. Since then, I have prepared an elixir in anticipation of just this situation. I need to administer the liquid now, so please go ahead and vomit and then we will get on with the remedy."

I held the bowl under his mouth as he proceeded to throw up only a small amount of dark-colored bile. There was nothing of substance in his stomach to bring up on which he might choke or aspirate, which was a relief.

As I took the small glass bottle of amber-colored dilution from my apothecary cabinet, along with a sterile dropper, I informed my patient, "Friedrich, I am going to place three drops of liquid under your tongue. It may burn slightly, but you must hold it there for two minutes. Do not swallow but breathe slowly through your nose as I count the minutes down."

He nodded and opened his mouth slightly as I quickly placed the dilution under his tongue. He closed his mouth, and I supported his jaw with gentle pressure to help ensure he would not swallow the medicine or spit it out.

"You are doing well. You have only thirty seconds left. Stay calm and still, focus only on your breathing," I said in a steady, soothing tone.

At the mark of one minute and forty seconds, he threw my hand from his chin, gasping for air and attempting to cough as he choked, panic enveloping him.

A slight dribble of saliva and elixir sputtered from his mouth, and I assumed the remainder had run down his throat, causing the choking. With the help of his men, we supported him into an upright position as I repeatedly encouraged him to calm himself.

"Commandant, your body now has the medicine, and by holding it under your tongue it is being quickly absorbed into your tissues." He finally caught some air, and I once again laid him back onto the pillows, his head and torso moderately elevated.

"I am going to bathe your body in lavender water while removing the barbs and double-checking to be sure all are gone from your skin. I'll then apply lavender honey to all your stings. I am also going to place a cool wet cloth of lavender water on your forehead and honey across your eyes. Again, you must stay calm."

"You cannot save me, Nurse. Let me die," he croaked, barely able to move his lips.

"You are not going to die, but you must help save yourself if you want to live."

Truth be told, the next thirty minutes would determine if his symptoms extended, and if so, there was little I could offer other than the elixir and my natural remedies to reduce his swelling and ease the pain.

After I applied soothing ointments to his body, I instructed his comrades to stay with him and then took myself over to Sister Dominique's desk to sit and calm my own person. I found myself trembling, not from worry regarding the condition of my patient but from worry that I was struggling with of my own. Since first appearing at my door today and seeing the serious state in which the commandant presented, I consciously forced my mind to a place of denial. I denied the part of me that hated this man and what he was about. I would not have grieved should he die as a result of his own stupidity. He was the one placing himself at known risk.

It was true, I could not save him, nor did the Frenchwoman in me want him saved. But so strong was my instinct to heal, to nurse, that it overrode my baser response to allow this man to suffocate and be done with him. I was glad for the presence of the other two soldiers, which perhaps reinforced my responsibilities as a nurse.

Needing air of my own to breathe, I walked to the clinic door and opened it. To my shock, there stood Henri, curled hand poised to knock.

"I heard the commandant is once again your patient. A very ill patient. Is there anything I can do to assist you?"

I stood looking at my friend, my sight clouded by sudden tears, my body once again shaking. Henri gently pulled me onto the small landing and into himself, closing the door quietly as I said softly, "I do not know that I can save him. I do not know that I want to."

"You will give your utmost, Nurse Durant. That is all you have to give and that is sufficient. It is ultimately his struggle. You must let yours go as well."

As I leaned back to wipe my eyes, all I could do was nod, knowing what Henri said was true. I did not want vengeance or retribution; it was everything I thought I firmly denied and not a true part of my soul. And yet this wrenching struggle was all too real and the conflicting desires between life and death so very strong. I nodded once more to let Henri know I had regained a semblance of control.

Giving him a look of resigned confidence, I said firmly, "I am composed now and I will finish with my patient." He understood and, knowing I needed to take care of this matter on my own, remained outside on the landing. I returned to my patient.

The commandant's breathing was ragged but he was resting quietly. I removed the damp cloth from his face, rinsed it once more in lavender water, and set it again upon his forehead. His eyes were closed as I gently applied more honey to the swellings.

"You boys can go sit in the chairs by the door." I turned to them. "Your commandant can do without you for a while now. Rest yourselves. And you, Commandant, can you tell me how you are feeling?"

"Wie die Hölle." He said these words slowly in a muted, harsh voice, his breathing shallow and raspy. But he was gaining sufficient air on inhalation to meet his needs.

"Of course you feel like hell. That is to be expected. Can you be more specific? Does your throat itch? Do you feel any tightness when you swallow? Do you think you could drink an infusion tea?"

"Yes, to all your damn questions. Am I to live?"

"You most likely will, unless you die of humiliation and stupidity. Or next time you may just die from anaphylaxis."

"I don't plan on a next time."

"Ah! A good indication that you are thinking rationally about a dangerous situation in which you intentionally placed yourself."

The general swelling of his joints had not extended and there was no recurring nausea. Over the many years of medical conversations and consultations with Tanvir, he often regaled the benefits of Indian green tea in helping to reduce inflammation and subdue the allergic histamine response in many patients. When deemed appropriate I, too, administered green tea to my patients, and it had become part of my arsenal of treatments. Therefore, I brewed a very strong pot of green tea steeped from whole leaves.

When the tea was ready, I instructed the commandant to drink it slowly, which he did, sip by slow sip. The tea has a bitter taste, especially when so strong; however, he did not choke or gag but did pause after every small swallow to take a breath. Taking again his blood pressure, pulse, and listening to his lungs further assured me his symptoms, though still significant, were not extending.

The commandant lay relatively calm and quiet for an hour before I administered a second dose of the *Apis mellifica* dilution. When another hour had passed, with his breathing and vital signs now stable and his mood as vile as ever, he insisted on leaving. I countered with an offer to stay in the clinic with him through the night should his symptoms recur and need immediate attention.

"There is nothing further I need except to leave your clinic. And I certainly do not need your permission to do so."

I made no argument, did not try to convince him to stay, but put together a packet of green tea leaves, lavender oil, lavender honey, and the small bottle of elixir with a dropper, accompanied by brief instructions for each item's use. He seemed to pay no mind to my words but did agree to return the following day.

With help from his fellows, I watched him hobble away to their vehicle. Between his limp and his stiff, swollen joints, the commandant was a man toppled by ego and insects. He was certainly still at risk but, for the moment, alive. My patient had a stronger will to live than my bees, or any of us, had desire to be rid of him.

CHAPTER 32

CLUES AND INTUITION – FALL 1943

While the arrests and deportations continued across France and the Allies began air raids over Paris, those in the cities again fled to the countryside. Once more, we were gleaning firsthand accounts of the devastation on every level of life that continued to ravage our country and its people.

In Meuse, we continued the struggle to maintain our self-sufficiency, our dignity, and to ignore the rumbles from both our stomachs and the planes overhead. Meat was virtually nonexistent and fresh bread had become a delicacy. Our clothes and shoes were barely adequate, but our stores of preserved foods were sufficient to keep the children fed. The lavender honey was doled out judiciously, and its summer sweetness was a reminder that we would be warm again come spring. With another winter approaching, being chilled to the bone became our constant but never our normal.

What little fuel could be found—coal, wood, or otherwise—we used prudently to cook or to warm the children. I treated many winter runny noses, coughs, and colds, but our hidden children remained, for the most part, whole and healthy. As we protected them all, our guiding hope was that when peace came, they would be strong enough to go on living their lives.

My clinic constantly accommodated a coming and going of peoples, a place of triage for the body and the spirit. Sustenance seekers from the cities crossed my doorstep many times to lay bare their concerns, often having me examine their children, as their never-ending concern was losing the ones most precious to them. For the most part, I could assure those anxious, hungry parents that their equally hungry children were fine.

While wanting to be generous, we were all needfully protective of our own limited provisions. Though I wished otherwise, I could not too frequently send people to the convent for food lest we became known as having an overabundance. The times were heartbreaking, and any fear I had of the Nazis, of the war in general, had long ago dissolved into angry frustration.

These last many months, I had seen little of Henri and Bernard, knowing they were engaged in their own affairs. The French Resistance was alive and well and filled the cold air of the coming winter with a breath of hope. It wasn't talked about openly, but we all supported efforts to stifle our occupiers in whatever ways we could. Men like Henri were players on a larger, though primarily covert, stage. When I did see him, stress lined his face, as if the weight of his secrets was as lead in the pockets of his soul. No, we did not talk about it. He would not, had I even inquired.

Every two weeks or so, when I made my way into town, we found time to share a meal with one another in his makeshift home in the back room of his business in Verdun. It was there that we found a semblance of privacy, a few moments apart from any other concerns to openly talk about what was most on our minds and in our hearts. When the weather permitted, we sometimes took walks along our river, sitting silently on its banks, our backs propped against the poplar trees. These occasions kept us connected to one another in this unsettled, angst-filled age. We were weary souls but often managed to find cause for laughter and always reason to hope.

My forty-seventh birthday had passed in October, taking along with it more of my vitality. During the days between my waning monthly menses, I would experience occasional bleeding, which was becoming more frequent and often heavier. Some days, there would be a lingering or recurring ache in my pelvis, mild but insistent, causing me to note its almost chronic presence. While I had counseled many women regarding the signs and symptoms of menopause and knew, of course, firsthand the monthly pelvic and muscle aches and pains of normal menses, this was something outside the norm.

For the most part, I paid no attention to these happenings in my body. The breakthrough bleeding was concerning, spotting and clots now and again, but certainly, in the short term, not life threatening. But my intuition nagged at me that there was more to my symptoms than what was considered normal. As a nurse, I knew I might be having ovarian cysts, but the pain did not seem intense enough, and there was not a cyclical monthly pattern to it. If the symptoms did not progress to the point of interfering with my clinic work or the quality of my busy life in general, I would continue to disregard what I sensed was most likely a progressive situation, for which there was little to be done, especially in these times of war. I did, though, plan to share my situation with Rose, wanting at least one other person to know should someone find me unable to explain.

Just after sunrise on a Sunday, ignoring the drops of cold rain, I harnessed Horse to the wagon. He was in need of exercise and I needed a diversion, so we set off for Lavender House. I had a basket full of canned goods hidden in the wooden trunk in the back of the wagon, which certainly wasn't a true hiding place for prying German eyes, but I did not expect to be stopped on this windy, wet fall day. For the most part, the commandant and his men left me to my habitual route back and forth from house to clinic, clinic to convent. My life was much too predictable and mundane to warrant their interest. How thankful I was for my boring ways and the commandant's fear of my bees that helped keep our children safe.

I was soaked through when Horse pulled the wagon up to Rose and Bernard's shed. I jumped down and led him into his stall, where I dried him with one blanket and covered him with another before taking my basket of jars and running through the rain to my house.

"Bonjour," I called quietly, stepping through the back door. I lined the jars in a neat row on the wooden counter, the colorful contents of red, yellow, and green looking quite festive.

"Marie!" said Rose, walking into the kitchen. "What a wonderful surprise. Take off those wet clothes while I get you something dry."

Rose was a woman of strong countenance with a compassionate nature. Upon seeing her slight frame and lovely features, one would describe her as a "delicate woman"—small and slender, her large gray-blue eyes, skin of porcelain, hair golden-blonde and full all belying her inner strength and cunning. What an effective disguise for a woman of such fortitude. I knew she bravely assisted Bernard's resistance efforts in some way, relishing even the slightest victory over our captors.

The children were still sleeping and not yet aware of my arrival, so I quickly ducked into a corner of the kitchen to peel off my garments. Rose brought me the extra trousers and a heavy wool shirt I kept at the house for just such occasions.

"And now, sit and I will make us tea and eggs. Why in the world are you out in this weather? We thank you for the food, but you did not need to come all this way on such a nasty day."

"I needed a respite from the concerns that keep swirling round and round my mind, a time here to center myself and see the little ones. And to spend time with you, Rose."

We sat at my table in the dining room under the window facing the Meuse. Rose poured our tea and offered me a hard biscuit with our scrambled eggs, which I left untouched on the plate, my cold hands wrapped round the warm cup.

"And the children?" I asked. "What is new with them all?"

"I spent yesterday letting down the hems of pants and dresses. By spring we will need to somehow find more old clothes to make new ones."

"It is the same at the convent school. The children are growing faster than the Sisters can sew for them, but we can pass some of the clothing along to the smaller ones. That is a wonderful thing. They are all as healthy as we can expect under such circumstances."

"And you? How are you doing under such circumstances?"

"I am keeping up with my patients and, if I am judicious, still have sufficient medical supplies for some time yet. Henri has them stashed somewhere he won't even tell me about but brings them to me as I ask."

I paused then, drinking most of my cooled tea before sharing the burden I came to unload. "I do have some physical issues that are causing me some discomfort and loss of energy. I wanted to talk with you about those."

"You have been looking very tired for some time, and I wondered if you were carrying more than you should. But is there something else, Marie?"

"There may be something brewing in my body that could become concerning. Initially I thought it was just symptoms of menopause and fatigue due to aging, but the past few months I am almost sure it is something more. There is recurrent bleeding, fatigue, weight loss, and pain in my pelvic area. Of course, the weight loss is normal for all of us right now, but this is more than would be expected. And I have noticed the lymph glands in my neck have been swollen for some time. I am thankful that no matter how deeply I palpate the glands under my arms or into my breasts I feel no swelling there. That is good news and perhaps whatever is growing is doing so very slowly."

"You sound like you are describing a patient of yours. For heaven's sake, Marie, what do you mean 'growing'? You think you have a growth of some kind? If so, why have you not gone to Paris and received treatment for whatever is wrong?"

Rose was always inordinately calm in all situations, but I knew her well enough that when the pitch of her voice rose slightly, she was moving toward either agitation or concern. I heard the concern in her voice and was relieved that I could share with her what I believed was happening to me.

"I'm not sure, but I think that I may have some type of cancer, such as abdominal or uterine. Because of the symptoms, I am thinking the latter."

"But this is terrible, Marie! You must go to Paris! Now! To your hospital there and get some answers."

"I am not interested in treatments that are often worse than the illness. Truly, Rose, I believe I will be most at ease letting things unfold as they will. There is no part of me that is afraid or feels a need for an evaluation. It must sound odd, but I feel an extreme sense of peace. I choose to remain in my clinic with my patients and here with our friends, dealing with whatever evolves. What better place to be if and when I can no longer practice?"

"Really, Marie, while your words are quite noble, I think your decision is foolish and very selfish. There is no one but you that will be 'at peace' with any of this. I can't leave the children, but I know Henri will accompany you to the hospital, and another set of eyes and ears would be helpful when talking with the doctors."

"That isn't going to happen, Rose. What I have shared with you is not to be shared with anyone else, especially not Henri or Bernard."

"What a burden to place on me. One I will reluctantly honor, but I don't appreciate being complicit in any of this. A medical professional not seeking help? Again, I think it selfish and very foolish of you."

"Perhaps. But it is my own life and therefore my decision entirely. If you prefer, we can pretend this conversation never occurred, and I won't bring up the issue again. I am very happy to do so and won't be offended in any way should that be your wish."

"And now you assume that you can't share your worries and concerns with me? Just because I don't agree with your decision? We have shared so much for so long, and there is no reason to change now. I reluctantly promise what you have told me will remain in confidence, but you must promise me as well that you will consider seeing a doctor. Maybe these symptoms are just what happens as we change, and since you haven't experienced them before, how would you know?"

"I know, and again, I am not at all worried about what lies ahead. We all have enough to worry us without my adding to the heap. I'm more than grateful for your friendship and willingness to listen, and, of course, I always appreciate your honesty."

"At least keep me informed as to how you are feeling. I promise I will listen and try not to give too much advice. You know that will be difficult, but truly, I will give you any support you need. Including not saying anything to Bernard or Henri."

Before I could answer, soft, sleepy sounds emanated from a small bed I had not taken note of before. Rose got up quickly and lifted the small swaddled bundle into her arms.

"Shhhh, Émile. We don't want to wake the others. Let's get your bottle, little one." She gently bounced what I assumed was a young babe into the kitchen. I followed her and watched as she filled a bottle with one hand while continuing to comfort the hungry child.

"Here, Rose, let me take him."

Rose handed the baby over, and as I lifted aside the corners of his blanket, I was met by a pair of lovely dark brown eyes, long-lashed and brilliant, and a head of blonde curls.

"And who might you be, little one? I do not think I have made your acquaintance," I said, and looked meaningfully at Rose.

Without making eye contact, Rose responded, "This is Émile. We think he must be about three months old."

"I thought Henri brought all the children first to me, to be sure they were healthy, with no risk of contagion to the other children. And I certainly would have remembered this darling boy. How did he come to be here?"

Rose sighed. "Come sit back at the table, Marie, and I will tell you all about Émile." Before we were even seated, she began her tale, speaking quickly as she fed the hungry baby.

"Three weeks ago, one of Bernard's errands in Verdun took him to a part of town that had that morning seen another neighborhood raid. Jewish families in hiding had been discovered and were taken away. Bernard went to see if he could find any trace of adults or children that may have escaped the soldiers. As he walked through an abandoned townhouse, he heard muffled cries and followed the sound. Apparently, someone had found enough time and the presence of mind to place this baby into the back of an armoire.

"Bernard took the child, hiding him in the folds of his large coat, and brought him directly home to me. We have been keeping the baby with us, Marie. I bring him to Lavender House during the day, and he goes home with me those nights when Philippa stays with the children. Bernard and I have decided to keep him and that his name is to be Émile."

Rose told me all this in a rush of words as the baby steadily sucked at the bottle, his small fingers entwined in hers, both of them holding onto each other as though for life.

"He certainly is precious, and it was indeed fortunate that Bernard found him alive. I can understand how you feel, that you want to make him your own child. But how will you and Bernard feel if you become so attached and then his family is found alive and he must be returned to them?"

"I do not know how Bernard knows but he said there is no chance his family survived. He would not say more when I pressed, other than that witnesses saw the people fight against their captors, that they resisted fiercely and were just as fiercely beaten in response. I believe many were killed in the raid, killed and their bodies thrown in a heap and taken away. Émile is all that is left of them."

Looking from the baby to me, with tears in her eyes, she said softly, "It was almost too late but still just in time. We already love him as our own. He is our own, Marie."

I rose and moved behind my dear friend, giving her shoulders a loving squeeze. This child was the epitome of hope in this dark time. His presence in all our lives would prove to be a soothing balm for our souls and a constant reminder to honor those that were lost.

The other children were beginning to wake now and clamor for attention. I hugged them each, helped Rose prepare their breakfast, and saw myself out the front door. I stood on the porch for a moment and gazed out at my beloved Meuse. Taking advantage of a reprieve in the downpour, I walked across the road to my river and strolled along its banks for perhaps thirty minutes. I kept examining my feelings, thinking about Rose's words, that I was selfish in not seeing a doctor. Yet the more I lay with my truth, the surer I was of the peace that filled my heart. Death was not anything I feared and was certainly no worse than what had been experienced through two wars and too much loss. I was weary now in all ways, finding strength only in the lives of our precious children.

CHAPTER 33

SALVATION – WINTER 1943

The onset of another winter brought with it even more famine and hardship for France. The shortage of food was extreme, and our hopes were pinned on the spring, when we could begin once again to plant our gardens. I had been aggressively treating my physical ailments homeopathically and was feeling better than I had in many months. Rose continued to be my confidante and was exuberant and convinced that I was much better, and all I needed was more rest and more good wine to "build my blood."

Every two weeks, I had taken to spending Saturday afternoon until Monday noon at Lavender House with the children. The time with them was my salvation, allowing me to face the withering hope that this war would ever end. Another war, once again desolating countries and people, another bid for power by men who sacrificed all that was sacred for their own prideful agendas.

As Horse and I approached Rose's house and I looked across the fields to my own, I saw no smoke from the chimneys. This was expected, since any sign of smoke would alert the Germans that the house was occupied. But the knowledge that no fires burned in my stoves in the dead of winter tore at my heart, knowing those within were terribly cold.

I settled my horse and walked through the fields to my house. Entering by the kitchen door, I was greeted by the pungent odor of farm animals and children accompanied by soft clucking, bleats, young laughter, and small feet running up and down the stairs in playful abandon. And my heart filled with gratitude for this respite in time.

The children looked forward to my visits and, knowing I always arrived with some treat for them, would scurry about me with sincere greetings and welcome hugs. The day before my journey home, I would ask the Sisters to bake a surprise, madeleines or cookies of some type, depending on what was in their sparse larder. Our ample supply of lavender honey always ensured whatever the creative women conjured up was sweet.

Henri worried that my extended visits would arouse suspicion and the commandant would seek out my whereabouts. The nuns were told to say I was visiting my good friend Rose Schultz and her family. That it was how I spent my much-needed free time away from the clinic. And, indeed, I did see my friend on these occasions. Rose continued her commitment, spending her days tending to the children, and I knew she would be there when I arrived on these Saturday afternoons.

I often suspected Commandant Reichenbach knew I was involved in something clandestine. He may even have known about the hidden children. But knowing he owed his very life to me, I chose to believe he looked the other way, and when he did look to see, it was through eyes of mercy rather than hate.

Four months after his terrifying episode with my bees, the commandant had come quietly to my clinic door. It was a Friday at dusk, and I had just completed my last patient appointment of the day. I had to assume he had been waiting till I was alone.

The knock upon my door was not his usual hard-fisted bang. The polite two knocks fooled me into thinking it was an acquaintance come to say hello or a late patient needing care. I opened the door with a smile that quickly receded when I realized it was not a welcome face.

"May I come in, Nurse Durant?" he asked, removing his hat.

"And would it be of any benefit to tell you no, that my day is done and I am on my way home to the convent?" I stepped aside, allowing him and the howling winter wind into the room.

"I will be brief and not keep you from your evening. I wanted to thank you again for your medical attention last summer. I have spent much time in contemplation and realize my situation was serious and I could have died."

I remained by the door, hoping his thank-you was all he came to say and that I could bid him a hasty goodbye. "Your situation was quite serious and should certainly serve as a dire warning to stay away from the bees. How are you feeling now?"

"Fully recovered, of course, but with questions."

"Medical questions? About the bee stings?"

"No. Questions about life and death." He sat himself down on one of the chairs beside the door and gestured me to do the same.

My heart sank but I sat, realizing there was more to this visit than a brief thank-you. He was silent for many seconds, moving his hat round and round with his fingers. Not imagining what he wanted to ask, I kept still, my hands folded calmly in my lap and my heart jumping in my chest with each gust of wind that rattled my door.

"You see, Madame Durant, I have thought for many years that death would be a welcome escape from a life of pain and loss. The military demands a man be unencumbered, and I have no one and nothing to tether me to any place. Other than my loyalty to my country and my Führer, I have nothing. Service to my country has saved me."

My ire was stirred instantly, and my words erupted without reservation. "You willingly extend loyalty to a monstrous human who sees himself as some savior figure? And what is he saving you from? Innocent people of other religions, other colors, and other philosophies? I would think you a more intelligent person, Monsieur, than one willing to live and die for an insane dictator. If that is your truth, your salvation, then I agree, you have nothing worthwhile to live for."

He seemed to ignore my words and took up where he left his thoughts. "But when I was stung this last time and fighting to breathe, I realized I did not want to die, and that puzzles me."

Before I could respond, the wind struck the clinic with such a fierce blast the door burst open. I jumped up quickly to close it. I welcomed the momentary distraction, attending to the storm's piercing voice rather than the commandant's. As the wind calmed, so did I, answering him in a voice intended to be resolute rather than accusatory. "Why do you think not wanting to die is the direct opposite of wanting to live? They are not always in opposition. The human mind is more complex than being either one way or the other. You have many choices. Do you stay away from bees and live or purposely go where they will sting you and possibly die? Do you live encumbered by hate and blind obedience or do you do what you can in the position you are in to prevent loss of life? Why is your life of greater value than another's? You have choices."

His eye began to twitch; he heard my stiff words. Rising out of his chair, he limped slowly toward my tapestry screens. His back was to me now as he hissed, "How dare you question the intentions of my country or how I choose to serve. You waste your time thinking anything you do will change the outcome of this war. Why do you and the others risk your souls when you have no means of salvation other than what we bestow on you? This country needs to accept our occupation as your future. Your future is now. You are the ones with no choices."

I stood slowly, silently watching him glide one rough hand across the delicate stitches of my embroidered silk cranes. The light in the room had dimmed, cloaking the space in ominous shadow. I purposefully walked to Sister's desk and removed the box of long wood matches from her middle drawer. Five thick beeswax candles were placed about the clinic, and I moved slowly round the room, lighting each one in turn. There was a long silence before I asked, "Did you fight in the Great War? Is that where you acquired your limp?"

Heaving a sigh as loud as the wind, he said, "Yes, I served in the fields of the Great War, but my injuries from that conflict were not physical. I had polio as a child and that is why I limp. I should have realized early on that life would be nothing but disappointment and pain."

The candles lit, I moved to my desk beside the silk screens and leaned heavily against its solid support. "Do not be naïve. Everyone suffers injury and pain of all sorts through their lives. No one is exempt. But everyone has a choice to rise each day, or at least most days, knowing they can begin again."

He looked hard into my eyes before returning to the chair by the door and easing himself onto it. "You are the naïve one, Madame, a fool to think anyone has choices."

"I could not be foolish and do my work, Commandant. I am, on most days, strong and realistic, and on most mornings I rise hopeful, even in the face of harsh reality."

He bent forward and, with his elbows on his knees, cradled his head in his hands. In a hollow voice, he asked, "Do you believe in fate? Predestination?"

I paused as the wind blew strong against the windows, finding gaps to sneak through. The candles' bright flames flickered wildly before flaring tall again as I thought of how to answer this man whom I did not trust but did not fear.

"We cannot always determine our destiny, but we can always choose how we respond to circumstances. That is where our freedom lies—in choosing how we react, how we respond to what life places in front of us. I admit that while I sincerely believe this to be true, I have much to learn in that regard."

"Are you religious, Nurse Durant?" His head still rested in his hands. The bald expanse at the top of his head, gleaming in the candlelight, reminded me of his vulnerability.

I sat down again on the chair beside him. "I told you, I am Catholic, and la Vierge Marie is to whom I pray."

His head jerked up, eye twitching mockingly as he said, "Ah, you and the other Sisters, held hostage by a fake philosophy. Religion is nothing but a panacea holding the weak captive."

"Do you not realize that you are held captive? You are but a pawn in a treacherous game played by your Führer. You are as maligned by those in Berlin as are your supposed enemies. You are told who to hate, who to kill, who to persecute, and who to fear. You have embraced an agenda of persecution and slaughter and on that you base a life worth living? Next time you put yourself in the way of my bees, do not come to me to save you."

Silence fell upon the room again. My heart was pounding. I was almost panting from angst and could hear my breathing, loud and strained.

He remained in the chair, staring across the room with vacant eyes. I could smell in his sweat the familiar acrid stench of fear, the smell that permeated battlefields of every conflict. "Then where is salvation, Madame?"

My next words were measured, knowing this man before me was in extremis, searching for answers and hoping mine would be salve to his soul. But I had only my truth to tell him.

"There is no salvation here, not in this room, not with me. And I am not a nun, not a holy woman but someone seeking forgiveness and truth, as we all are. And I would rather live in hope than die of despair. That is the choice we all have."

"Again, you know nothing of my choices, Nurse—you and your pious friends!" He tossed his head and, looking down his nose at me, said, "All of you creating a constant brouhaha instead of gratefully accepting the inevitable. You think you know the ending and that it will be a happy one? I say again, you have no choices, much the same as me."

I was weary of this man's weak rage, his vacillating emotions, and weary as well of my own feelings of futility. "Neither of us may have much control regarding our present circumstances, but we can choose to hope that sanity will ultimately prevail and this exhausting war will end.

"How can you, an educated woman, sit there and talk of hope? Hope! How can you possibly believe in a God who once again condemns us to a living hell?" Attempting to rise quickly, he lost his footing and stumbled against the wall. With great effort, he regained his composure and turned around to me with a haunting despair in his eyes. He gave a curt nod in my direction and abruptly donned his hat then quickly fled the clinic, struggling against the wind to close the door on his way back into the darkness.

I still sat there, tears pooling at the edges of my eyes as my heart began to slow. The commandant's fearful look of deep anguish lingered, causing me to acknowledge that this brittle man was standing on the edge of a great emotional precipice. He came to me thinking I would provide spiritual care as I had cared for him physically. But my words were true. I could offer him no semblance of salvation.

The next day at noon, I returned to Lavender House. As always, the children brought solace to my own weary soul. After an afternoon of playing games and welcome conversation with Rose and Philippa, I fell upon my cot into a troubled sleep, the contentious visit with the commandant still on my mind.

Sometime close to midnight, the wind calmed and the sky cleared. I awoke to the full moon's bright light shining round the edges of the dining room's window coverings. It irresistibly beckoned me to come give witness to its powerful beauty. Rising from my bed, I quietly donned my wool coat, boots, gloves, and scarf and stepped outside onto the back stoop.

The moon was suspended high and magnificent, with a haloed aura of silver brilliance circled round itself. A new snow had fallen. The fresh flakes shined luminescent under the celestial light, creating a blanket of glittering jewels over the sleeping lavender fields. Only the tips of the dormant bushes were visible, the beehives standing as tall sentinels watching over the beautiful moonlit landscape.

In this place where I stood, I was hidden from all the world, alone in absolute silence—absolute solitude and suspended in peace. Breathing the frigid air, I felt cleansed, encased in a cold hibernating slumber as the land patiently awaited a warm summer sun as bright as this winter moon. A brilliant light of hope in this time of darkness.

Worry had been my constant companion, and I cloaked it in continuous complaints about the long, frozen winters. I thanked the moon for the reminder that there are always winter seasons in life, some harsher than others . . . that these difficult times require us to hibernate and wait with fortitude and patient hope for a coming season of renewal.

I thanked the moon for her wisdom and took myself inside to a peaceful sleep.

CHAPTER 34

LIBERATION – SEPTEMBER 1944

We were at Lavender House the day the Allies moved into Verdun and the Germans retreated. But their exit was not without penalty. Verdun was heavily bombed following Patton's victory entrance into the city, and for days after, German planes continued dropping bombs, devastating the town.

The Germans had done extensive damage to Verdun during their hasty exit, shelling as much infrastructure as they could manage to destroy. On their way out of town, they placed explosives along the river's bridge, hiding the triggering mechanisms in surrounding trees. Fortunately, members of the Resistance discovered the plot and climbed the trees along the river, disarming the firing mechanisms and throwing the explosives into the Meuse.

Even as we took a deep breath of liberated relief, we were once again left with the detriment of war—heaping mounds of pillage and destruction all around us. We were all more than exhausted. Knowing we were faced with years of recovery felt daunting and frustrating in every conceivable way. But the invaders were gone, our bridge was preserved, and our country was free.

Several days before the liberation of Paris, on 25 August, Commandant Reichenbach went missing. The Allies were moving steadily toward Verdun, and the Nazis were preparing their retreat. I only knew of the commandant's disappearance because several of his soldiers went door to door, canvasing Verdun and the surrounding countryside, looking for their commanding officer.

Arriving at my clinic early one morning, I asked them what everyone else had assumed for days now. "Do you not think your commandant has fled in the face of defeat? Left France posthaste?"

"He would never abandon his men, Madame. We talked many times about what retreat would look like: he was to lead us out. He is not a coward."

I tended to agree with his loyal soldiers. Friedrich Reichenbach would never have voluntarily left his men to flee without him but would have led the retreat from France.

"I am sorry that I cannot provide you with any information. He has not appeared at the clinic in need of any medical assistance. If he had, you would have been notified and instructed to take him with you on your way out of our country. I have heard nothing about his whereabouts nor seen him in many days."

They left quickly, headed back toward Verdun and still driving Henri's car, which I had no doubt they would take with them or destroy before leaving.

As the Allies neared Verdun, I learned that the commandant was still not accounted for nor seen among the retreating Germans. I found my curiosity piqued, wondering where Reichenbach could be. If anyone knew, it would be Henri and Bernard, and they would never say. If anyone else knew, it would be Rose. The next day, I decided to climb aboard Horse and pay my dear friend a visit.

Upon arriving at her home, I was not surprised to find her door ajar and tea in preparation. Our friendship had grown stronger, our bonds closer over this past year as we worked together caring for the children. Every month or so, Rose would also inquire after my physical concerns. Today being no exception, we seemed to sense when one might seek out the other.

"Bonjour, Rose."

"Bonjour, Marie. Émile is sleeping soundly, and I am just sitting down with tea," she said, taking another cup and saucer from her neatly organized kitchen shelves. I sat down on one of the long wooden benches at her kitchen table, the same table she had in this small, rustic three-room home the first time I met her.

That day, Bernard had come to the clinic needing care for his own person, and as he was leaving almost forgot to inform me that Rose's husband, Jacob Weir, told him his wife was having a great deal of difficulty delivering their second child. She had been in labor for two days and seemed to be doing poorly and in need of help. After admonishing Bernard for not telling me as soon as he entered the clinic, I hastily gathered linens, supplies, and my medical bag. We jumped into Bernard's truck and immediately set out for the Weirs'.

At the end of that long day, four-year-old Hélène was joined by a second girl, extremely small and weak. The entire family was ill, which made Rose's delivery of her fragile baby even more difficult. Jacob, having returned home from the first war greatly damaged in spirit and finding only sporadic work, had done little to care for his family or their home. They were barely surviving. With another mouth to feed, the tragic souls were now in real danger of dying from malnutrition and despair. Bernard and I nursed them for many weeks after ridding them and their house of lice and treating their conjunctivitis and malnutrition.

During those days of recovery, Jacob physically and emotionally distanced himself; we saw him but a few times a long way off in the fields, alone. Months later, little Hélène found the father she adored hanging from a tree, his damaged soul at peace but his family now completely abandoned by this tortured man. Three days later, the baby passed as well. Bernard, bless his heart, stepped in to ensure that Rose and her young daughter had food, wood for their stove, and whatever else they needed to sustain life.

Bernard and Rose married two years later, much to the dismay of Hélène, who continued to mourn her father. Bernard kept his own house and farm, and Rose and Hélène continued to live in her little cottage with its bare wooden floors and meager but adequate furnishings. They insisted the arrangement suited them all perfectly. And now they were indeed content with their lives, including Sister Hélène in her life as a nun and teacher in the convent school.

Rose put the stoneware dishes down in front of me and returned to the stove, saying, "I made early biscuits and there are plenty for us to have with our tea."

Taking up a thick cloth serving pad, she removed the pan from the oven and put four golden biscuits on a plate, which she set on the table between our saucers. She left those remaining atop her counter and brought a jar of lavender honey and a small slab of butter to the table while I found two knives and *serviettes*, and we sat down to enjoy our mid-morning treat. How odd it seemed, to be enjoying this moment in time when our country was at loose ends, only just beginning to understand that the Allies had arrived, and we had been liberated. It seemed a confused dream following a tortuous nightmare.

We ate in silence for several minutes, more tea being poured before I commented, "Now that the Germans are gone, we can open the house freely and attempt to find the parents of the children. I suspect it will take quite some time for us to find information, if any is to be found at all. Of course, the children can stay in my home as long as needed. And I hope, Rose, that you and Philippa might consider continuing with their care as you have been."

Licking the dripping honey from her long fingers, she said through a mouthful of biscuit, "Of course we will. The little ones are as my own. But what will we do if their families cannot be located?"

"Let us meet that obstacle when and if it arises. We have greater things to be concerned about today. Such as how to keep filling our stomachs. I am so thankful that our hidden gardens will provide a good harvest this season, and I'm certainly looking forward to moving the chickens, rabbits, and goat outside and doing a thorough cleaning and airing of the house. And now we can begin thinking about expanding our numbers of animals as well as vegetables."

"Ha-ha, I agree! Perhaps we can move the animals outside tomorrow. Won't it be lovely to have a clean-smelling house for us all!"

We finished our cups of tea before I asked mildly, "Have you heard the commandant has gone missing? Hasn't been seen for many days. It seems peculiar that he would leave his men ahead of their formal retreat."

Rose flicked her right hand in the air dismissively. "What do we care? Only that he has left, along with all his despicable soldiers. I give him not one second thought."

"You know I nursed him, saved his life actually, when he was near fatally stung by my bees. I expended a great deal of effort on that man and would at least like to know what happened to him."

Rose, attempting to wipe her sticky fingers on the napkin, cocked her head with a sly look. "And you think *I* know? You think *I* would know what has become of the man?"

"If anything surreptitious occurred, I am certain Henri and Bernard would know, and I have little doubt that Bernard, given his extreme hatred of the man, would gleefully share knowledge of the situation with you, Rose."

"Perhaps," she said lightly, her eyes glancing out the window for a second, "but that is not the case. I only know that he's disappeared. And what concern should it be to us? I, for one, am just relieved they are gone, and I care not how they left us."

The next day, an excited patient informed me that the commandant's body had been found, alone, some time dead and sitting stiffly upright in his chair in my favorite café in the center of Verdun—the café where I first saw the man. Apparently, the bullet hole through his forehead killed him instantly. My patient reveled in the story, relating with animation bordering on giddiness that the commandant's revolver was still on his person and not a shot had been fired from its chambers, proving he was "rightly killed by one of our brave men."

I finished hurriedly with the man, closing the door behind him and securing the bolt. Stunned but not surprised, I could not begin to take regard of the array of my emotions. I went back to my desk and sank slowly into my chair. My mind filled with thoughts of the futility of war. The commandant was gone, his struggles ended. Deep sadness filled my soul at the thought of all the thousands and thousands perished over the last years and just as many remaining who would struggle to find some meaning to it all. As in the last war, many would never recover.

I pictured the commandant again and felt regret round the edges of my grief. Regret that I had not said more to reassure him, that my words had been harsh and cutting—of no comfort whatsoever. But they were words of truth, my truth as I knew it, which was all I could offer him then. I prayed that in death he found the salvation he sought in this life.

During those heady first days of victory, relief was our overriding emotion, our wills and spirits too expended to be celebratory. And the fact that we owed our freedom to other countries rather than our own French military slightly abraded my French pride. Without the allied soldiers, their munitions, and planes, we would not now be a free France once again.

CHAPTER 35

CLEANSING THE HOUSE – SEPTEMBER 1944–1946

Amazing how the mind and emotions can override physical ailments of the body. I felt some renewal of strength as, three days after my visit with Rose, with the Germans completely gone from Meuse, we excitedly emptied Lavender House for a good purging. It was another liberation of sorts, for the children were allowed to run free in the sun, the chickens dashed about pecking anything they thought might be edible, and the goat meandered through the tall stalks of purple flowers, munching as she went. Rose, Bernard, Philippa, Henri, and I carried the animal pens, much of the furniture, and all of the bedding outside to be washed, aired, and cleansed by the sun.

Inside, we scrubbed the floors, wiped down the walls, scoured the heavy metal bathtub, and all the chamber pots. While Henri and Bernard cleaned the pens, Rose and I took down all the curtains and window coverings, washing them in the now-shining bathtub before hanging it all to dry on a long rope Bernard had secured from a corner of my shed to a heavy hook he screwed in next to the kitchen door. It was heavenly, the heady sense of freedom allowing us to cleanse and begin anew. I felt renewed as well, hopeful and excited.

Though the afternoon was quite balmy, we built fires in both my upstairs and downstairs stoves and in the kitchen stove as well, allowing everything inside to dry thoroughly. Before dusk, we moved the furniture and the children's beds back in.

Everyone was invited to stay and eat. Bernard had brought along such a large amount of lamb shanks it looked like we were in store for a feast, which Rose browned in a heavy roasting pan with thick slices of onion and sprigs of rosemary. Giving it all a healthy dose of red wine and adding halved potatoes freshly dug from the garden, she placed it into the hot oven. While Rose was putting the finishing touches on dinner, I made up the children's beds with the extra linens.

And we had an added surprise. Henri informed me, with a twinkle in his eye, that he was heading to fetch the children from the convent school and all the Sisters. He and Horse delivered one wagon load of precious ones and Sister Hélène then returned to the convent for the rest of the Sisters. A short time later, we were all whooping and hollering as Ronan came roaring down the road, driving Henri's car—the one I thought surely was lost to him forever. And who but Félicité and Eugénie were with him, holding onto their hats, their scarves flying about their faces as the good Father honked the horn and drove past my house and back again before stopping in front of my steps.

"Ronan! Where on earth did you find my car? I thought it was well out of France by now!"

"The soldiers abandoned it before they reached the border. They drove it headlong into some dense shrubbery, disassembled the spark plugs, and ripped out wires. It has enough scratches and dents to say it, too, went through the war yet somehow survived."

"But how did you get ahold of it?" Henri asked.

"A farmer came to the church to find me. He recognized your car but couldn't find you so he told me. Together, we secured a heavy chain from his old tractor to your injured car, pulled it out, and towed it back to town. I've spent the better part of two days putting this thing back together for you, Henri. No telling how much you owe me for my services," he added, laughing.

"Merci beaucoup, good man! *C'est formidable!*" Henri said, slapping Ronan on the back. They then fell into a hug, laughing and joking with one another, tears making their way down each of their cheeks. None of us had dry eyes as we stood there lauding the efforts of these two good men to bring about more evidence of hope to this day.

When Rose confirmed what our noses told us, that dinner was ready, we decided to eat outside on blankets that we hurriedly laid upon the ground. The late September evening was almost warm, and the light still lingered as we consumed a veritable feast from stores still lining the convent's cellar shelves: canned beans and berries, fresh carrots and ripe tomatoes from our gardens, and the Sisters brought sweets. Rose's lamb shank was the best thing I ever tasted, for it tasted like freedom.

One by one, as the sun inched toward the horizon, the younger children dropped themselves into our laps and drifted off to sleep. The older ones played riotous games of chase, hiding from one another among the rows of lavender. Happy day!

As the last light began to fade, Ronan and Hélène rounded the older children into the buckboard wagon, harnessed up Horse, and carted them back to the convent school. Félicité and Eugénie rode on the high seat next to Ronan, the smiles on their faces broad with the anticipation of a wagon ride back to town. Henri and Bernard carried the sleepy little ones inside to their beds, where Rose, Philippa, and I tucked them in before Rose left to walk home with Émile. Philippa quickly fell asleep in her usual bed among the children. Henri, Bernard, and I remained at the house, moving to the quiet of the kitchen and seating ourselves at my old wooden table. The three of us needed to talk, and I would then stay the night.

"There are organizations, Jewish organizations, poised and ready to begin the process of reuniting lost children with their families," Henri began. "I propose we continue to keep the children here and at the school, caring for and educating them just as we have been. Who knows how long it will be until an accurate accounting can be done and people begin looking for relatives. I have already contacted two agencies in Reims, letting them know the names of our children, their Jewish names. I retained all documents the children had on them, if any, when they were brought to us or found."

"It should help that the older children remember their families—the names of their parents and relatives. Hopefully even addresses of where they lived. It won't be so easy to reunite the youngest ones with mothers and fathers. Did any of the little ones come with papers, Henri? Birth records or a document from anyone?"

"You are right, Marie. Most of the youngest ones ended up on our doorstep with minimal or no information of where they had lived. Certainly more of a challenge, but remember, families will contact the agencies, and we will have given them what information we have, including physical descriptions of all the children.

"I expect, in the event the children's parents cannot be located in whatever timeline the agencies deem sufficient, they will attempt to place them with Jewish relatives or in Jewish homes as they continue to search. Are we all in agreement that we will carry on as we have been, both here and at the school? The difference is that now we can care for the children openly and let our neighbors know we will gratefully accept any clothing or food they might want to contribute."

Bernard nodded his head. "I really don't know what Rose will do when she doesn't have this brood to care for. I know she is in no hurry to see them gone."

I smiled at Bernard. "Of course, we will all continue as we have been. If you let the agencies know who our children are, then we will wait for instructions from them. I think it best not to say anything to the youngest ones, as many will most likely not remember their previous lives. As for the older children at the school, can you ask your contacts at the agencies, Henri, what they feel is best? Are the children to be told there are efforts to reunite them with family or do we wait until there is actual information that their families have been located?"

"Another good question. Of course, once some of the older children have found their families, all of the children will be eager to be reunited as well. These next months will prove hard for us all. We'll wait to see how the reuniting process unfolds. At least we can actively move about without fear of repercussions. We need to also be aware of any persons coming back to the area looking for relatives, for children, that we may be able to assist."

Henri drove off in his restored car and Bernard walked home to Rose. Feeling quite exhausted, I was ready to retire for the night. I checked again on each sleeping child, placing my hand on their lovely heads and saying a prayer to la Vierge Marie that their parents would be found alive and well. The three of us had not touched on the very real possibility that many of their parents and other family members were lost forever.

• • •

Although the war waged on in other parts of the world, a free France moved steadily through the remaining months of 1944 and into 1945. Food and household items that we had before the war remained scarce all across the nation. We in the countryside continued to be thankful for the bounty of our gardens and our beehives full of summer honey. Bernard increased his numbers of livestock and generously shared hare, lamb, and chicken for meat, and we shared the generous offerings of our chickens' eggs. And as our community shared with us, we in turn shared with them. Day by day, month by month, restoration continued.

Félix and Solange had written numerous times, and though their letters and telegrams gave us constant joy, due to the still-disrupted postal and wire services, they were received long after they were written. My New York family were all well and extremely relieved to hear from us. Félix, now a physician surgeon in a New York hospital, was eager to return home. Henri and I were equally eager to be reunited with our son but instructed him to carefully consider whether he truly wanted to leave his life and work in New York. I did not tell my family that I was in failing health.

As the war continued throughout Europe and Asia, we followed the victories of the troops and Allies, along with the revelations of the horror inflicted by the Nazis. Once Auschwitz was liberated, in January of 1945, the world could no longer deny that the unimaginable had indeed occurred. At concentration camps throughout Europe, millions of Jews had been exterminated—men, women, children, babies, whole families—a staggering number.

By late 1945, with the ongoing efforts of the International Red Cross and the Jewish relief organizations registering the living and accounting for the dead, some of our children were reunited with their loved ones. The school saw five of the ten children rejoin their families, including Luc, Élise, and Michel. We sadly never heard any reports regarding Michel's younger sister, Camille, and this grieved all of our hearts.

Of the ten younger ones at Lavender House, now between the ages of six and nine, the agencies traced only two of the children to living relatives. In the midst of joyful reunion, there remained constant, sad despair at the reality of so many never to be reunited with family.

We continued working with the Jewish agencies, gladly caring for and educating the twelve children that remained with us. It was agreed that until permanent homes could be found, and because they were now all over the age of six, they would all stay together at the convent school. Philippa joined Sister Hélène in the full-time care of the children, the two women facilitating studies, activities, outings, and events. Rose and Émile were weekly visitors, and the children remained surrounded by love and constant support by us all. The agencies now knew that many of us who had sheltered and cared for them during the war were Jewish as well, that their heritage and religion was respected and acknowledged. Little by little, we continued the restoration of our own lives, albeit not always as we would have chosen.

My body, however, was not to be restored. As the year moved quickly along, I slowed down in equal measure. By the beginning of 1946, I moved more slowly through my days, thankful that I lived to see, hopefully, this last war come to an end.

Henri, our friends, and the Sisters knew that despite the reality that I was not going to heal, I was determined to continue with my patients for as long as possible. They also knew my state of being wasn't a subject I wanted to discuss. However, letting Félix and Solange know the state of my failing health was another matter. I took pen in hand and wrote a letter to Félix and a separate note to Solange, telling them that I was seriously ill, and sent it off. How I hated to surprise them with such news, especially in light of our victory. While I was not at all concerned by my own foreseeable passing, I knew it would greatly grieve their hearts.

CHAPTER 36

DEAREST BOY – JANUARY 1946

January 1946

My Dearest Boy,

How glorious that I can again write to you and the family in New York. I truly hope that you and everyone there is in good health. I am so very eager to hear all your news—everything that has been happening to you. I find myself needing to let you know that I have some news as well that I hope will not leave you distraught, as I am not distraught myself.

Since the summer of 1943, I have begun to feel less like myself, but being a woman of a certain age, I assumed it was normal and similar to what I had observed in so many of my female patients as we transition and age. However, as the months passed, I realized that my symptoms were likely those of a more serious nature and most probably cancer.

During the time since, as I have experienced increased pain and weakness, I shortened the hours of my clinic duties to rest and enjoy activities I had long since abandoned, painting being the pastime I now most enjoy.

I am sorry, my son, to tell you I will most likely pass away in the next few months or so. Please, please, Félix, do not worry yourself on my account. If you cannot, for any reason, return before I take my leave, it is not to be a concern of yours. I am in little pain and still managing on my own at Lavender House. There are more than enough people assisting me should things become more difficult. Henri, Rose, and the Sisters take much better care of my person than I ever did. My heart is at peace and I am filled with contentment.

You do know that I am always with you and no place more so than in this house and the clinic. For, again, both are yours, Dr. Félix Durant, and should you decide to take up your life here again in France or remain in America, that is your decision alone, my son. The house will always be here. I would be happy only if you are, and therefore, you must choose what makes your life fulfilling. And know that if you make one choice and it is not what you believed it would be, then you are completely free to make another. You will find life to be neither black nor white, but mostly gray, with patches of bright hope.

Please give my abiding love to Solange, Philippe, and Lilith, and let them know I feel their love and prayers. Your Oncle Henri, as always, is here by my side and sends his fondest regards to you all as well.

Do you know how very proud we are of you, Félix? A physician! And above that, one of the most wonderful souls ever created. My heart bursts with my every thought of you. How honored I have been to have you grace my life and my heart. Live well, my dearest son, and may your world be one of peace for all your time.

Forever Your Maman

January 1946

Dear Maman,

As soon as I received your letter, I booked airline flights home. I will be there soon, certainly before this letter reaches you. Maman. Please wait for us.

Forever Your Son,
Félix

CHAPTER 37

PASSAGES – FEBRUARY 1946

By February, Marie remained at home, finding solace and solitude in her beloved Lavender House. Her pain was gaining ground over her tenacity.

In November, she had shortened her clinic hours to four a day, twice a week. Her patients in many ways were keeping her on her feet, literally keeping her going from one day to the next, determined to continue her work. When attending to her patients became more arduous, we all assisted in any way she allowed. Two of the Sisters (one always Sister Dominique) walked with her slowly and carefully from the convent to the clinic and back again. Bernard made sure to clear any snow, creating a wide path in the road that she might walk more safely. And walking was, of course, what she insisted upon.

At the end of December, to our great relief, Marie decided it was expedient both for her patients and herself that she refer them now to the physician in Verdun. She wanted to go home to Lavender House, spending these last days with friends and family.

"I would like to have my bed placed in front of the window in the dining room. The table and chairs can just be moved closer into the parlor. Do you not think that is a fine idea, Henri?"

Taking her hand, I said sincerely, "Oui, ma chère, I do. I still see you sitting under that window all those years ago sewing your aprons together piece by piece."

"And all our talks there, Henri, all our meals with Félix, and those years with the children running all round the house. Yes, I am ready to just be settled at home and to remember. I will move to my memories. You know I am much at peace. My only wish is to see Félix. There is so much to tell him."

"He'll be here soon. I am sure he has much to share with us as well."

After Bernard, Rose, and I set the house up according to Marie's requests, the three of us gathered in the parlor, looking across to the bed that now stood against the wall under the west window toward the river. We sat there looking at that bed, waiting for Marie. On 24 December, gathering her from her beloved clinic for the last time, I brought her home.

Her voice still strong, her steps somewhat hesitant, and her attitude one almost of joy, Marie entered her Lavender House with a sigh of gratitude. "It is so very good to be home, knowing I never have to leave again. Thank you for all the trouble in getting me settled. I can admit that it is a great relief to just come home and be. These days will be ones of rest and reflection, and Bernard, I want to hear no complaints about anything. And Rose, no coddling me and I promise not to whine."

We laughed softly, knowing she meant all she shared. The peace and relief that showed on her face was a great comfort to me. My heart was aching, but I knew hers was full and ready to fly on.

Sister Dominique moved in with Marie, regularly administering the medication to keep the pain at bay and sleeping close by on the parlor's divan. The other Sisters visited in turn, as did Philippa. Between Bernard, Rose, and I, we were able to keep the numbers of good-intentioned well-wishers, so many of her patients and friends, from overwhelming her. I knew she wanted to preserve any strength remaining for Félix. I prayed he would arrive soon.

"Should I leave before he arrives, Henri, you know what to say."

"Of course I do! You have only made me recite it one hundred times, my dear. But you will be able to tell him yourself."

Félix, Lilith, and Solange arrived at Marie's door on a blisteringly cold, sunny afternoon in mid-January. Félix hurried to his mother and sat beside her on the bed, bursting with his arrival news. He filled the room with his energy and spoke so quickly Marie could hardly keep up with his words.

"Maman, we are here and all will be well. And I brought you two surprises."

188 · THE LAVENDER BEES OF MEUSE

"Ha-ha! You are truly here! My handsome Félix! Oh, how very wonderful to see you. Sit me up so I may truly look at you and we can talk."

As Félix and I helped her sit, Solange appeared in the doorway, a smile on her face and tears in her eyes.

She knelt beside the bed and gently took Marie's hand in hers. "And what is all this about, my sister? Have you not learned that you cannot keep secrets from me or I will come and scold you?"

Tears of joy and sadness in both their eyes, Marie wrapped her thin hands around Solange's. "Never, dearest sister, did I think I would see you again. My subterfuge worked! I brought you home once more. Henri, would you please put all my pillows behind me that I might better see the future?"

After making her as comfortable as we could, Félix eagerly turned toward the kitchen and motioned to a young woman to come into the room. Smiling through his own tears, he announced with great pride, "And Maman, this is your niece, Lilith. She is also your daughter-in-law . . . my wife. And a nurse, as you are! You remember, I told you how like you she is."

"Lilith, daughter of my sister and wife to my son? What a wonderful day this is! I can hardly take it all in. Henri, do you see that we have a daughter?" Marie exclaimed, holding her hands up to take Lilith's.

"I have wanted to meet you forever, Maman Marie. I am just so sorry it is under such sad circumstances."

"Oh, these circumstances would indeed be sad if you were all not here to make my leaving so joyful! How long have the two of you been married?" Marie asked, looking from Félix to Lilith and then at Solange with knowing eyes.

"Almost a month now, Maman, just before we decided to come home to France. It was a small ceremony—just the family and a few friends at Aunt Solange's and Uncle Philippe's. We were more eager to return home than anything. Now that we are here, we can truly begin our lives."

"I do hope you will not find life here too slow. It's much different than New York City. But as I told you in my letter, Félix, you must settle where it makes you happy, be that here or anywhere else."

"Coming home to Meuse is our hearts' desire, Maman, and with your blessing, Lilith and I hope to continue your practice at la Clinique Meuse." Félix's eyes were now overflowing with tears as he looked at Marie expectantly. "What would you think of that, Maman?"

"I think my heart is going to burst with joy." Marie looked from Félix to Lilith, her happiness evident in her broad smile. "And you both know this house is yours as well. To live in or not as you choose."

"Oui, Maman. That is our hope. This will indeed be our home, your Lavender House, and we promise to do both the clinic and this wonderful home great honor. You will be with us always."

· · ·

On 14 February, Marie passed just after sunrise, with the cocks crowing a new day. A short time later, I looked across to the river, not surprised at the sight of two graceful cranes flying languidly side by side over the placid flowing water of the Meuse. We sat with her for many hours after, each of us recalling our own memories, recalling all of who she was.

She was always my beloved.

HISTORICAL PERSPECTIVES

LOST CHILDREN OF THE SHOAH

Shoah is the Hebrew word for "catastrophe," and it specifically refers to the killing of Jews by the Germans during World War II, between the years 1941 through 1945. Of the six million Jews killed during the Shoah, or Holocaust, almost 1.5 million were children. Thousands of children survived because they were hidden.

Many of the children that escaped the killing centers and concentration camps did so due to the protection of people and institutions of other faiths. Jewish organizations such as the Jewish Health Society, the Federation of Jewish Societies, and the Zionist Youth Organization began underground efforts to place children with French families. Catholics and Protestants throughout Western Europe also hid Jewish children in their homes, orphanages, and schools. In Albania and Yugoslavia, Muslim families hid children as well. Catholics and Protestants, mostly through the church, succeeded in relocating half of the Jewish children in Paris to rural areas or in getting them out of France altogether.

Hiding Jewish children required all involved to maintain strict secrecy. Foster families created elaborate stories to explain the presence of new household members, most often saying the children were relatives. In some countries, such as the Netherlands, children were moved from place to place, often more than a dozen times, to help ensure their safety. Some convents and orphanages sought to secure new identification documents showing the children were not Jewish—that they had been baptized into the Christian faith. The hiding of children in *The Lavender Bees of Meuse* is a fictionalized account of children being given to the Catholic church in Paris by their parents or others in a desperate effort to save their lives. The children were then clandestinely transported to the churches in rural France. In the case of this story, Father Aubrey would receive the children at the cathedral in Verdun, some of whom were passed over to Henri. With the help of Marie, Bernard, and others, the children were then hidden in the Lavender House or placed under the protection of the Catholic church's convent school in Meuse.

Shortly after the war ended, in 1945, Europe's remaining Jews quickly began the arduous task of searching for and reuniting surviving family members. Tracing efforts were set up by Jewish relief agencies and organizations as well as the International Committee of the Red Cross, and the Joint Distribution Committee to find, unite, and place surviving children with found parents, relatives, or other Jewish families. Many surviving children of the Shoah lost not only their families but also their heritage and religion—their very essence. May we always remember what was lost in so many ways to war's anathema. May we honor these lost children and those who sacrificed to save them.

Resources:

"Children during the Holocaust," the website of the United States Holocaust Memorial Museum, Holocaust Encyclopedia, https://encyclopedia.ushmm.org/content/en/article/children-during-the-holocaust.

"Life in the Shadows, Hidden Children and the Holocaust," the website of the United States Holocaust Memorial Museum, Holocaust Encyclopedia, https://encyclopedia.ushmm.org/content/en/article/life-in-shadows-hidden-children-and-the-holocaust.

Krell, Robert, "Child Survivors of the Holocaust: 40 Years Later." *Journal of the American Academy of Child Psychiatry* 24, no. 4 (July 1985): 377–412.

HISTORY OF HOMEOPATHY

Homeopathy, the practice of treating disease based on the premise that the body can cure itself when given small doses of highly diluted natural substances, has been both hailed as highly effective and maligned as completely fraudulent.

In 1807, Samuel Hahnemann, a German physician, coined the term "homeopathy" or the "Law of Similars." These same methods for treatment of disease have been described in many cultures throughout history, including Mayan, Chinese, Greek, East Indian, and Native American. However, Dr. Hahnemann was the first to codify the Law of Similars into what practitioners of homeopathy believe is a systematic medical science.

During the 1900s, orthodox western medicine and pharmaceutical companies viewed homeopathy as a threat. They believed there was no strong scientific data to support the claims that homeopathy was an effective method of treatment for disease. Homeopathic physicians disputed these assertions, citing the high cure rates of their patients. These disputes continue today, with proponents and supporters in both camps.

France has a long history of utilizing homeopathic remedies, which can be found in pharmacies throughout the country. Marie was certainly a proponent of homeopathic and other natural herbal and plant-based interventions.

As described in *The Lavender Bees of Meuse*, during World War II, physicians and nurses in occupied France had little access to conventional medicines for the treatment of disease. Marie, who was introduced to homeopathic methods during her schooling in Paris, readily turned to compounding the *Apis mellifica* to treat the commandant's anaphylaxis. Other remedies used in successfully treating her patients' symptoms and illnesses included ointments with lavender and honey, herbal poultices, and infusions of herbal teas.

Resources:

Hahnemann, Samuel, *Organon of Homoeopathic Medicine: The Classic Guide Book for Understanding Homeopathy – the Fifth and Sixth Edition Texts, with Notes*. Translated by R. E. Dudgeon and William Boericke. CreateSpace Independent Publishing Platform, 2018.

"Homeopathy," the website of Dr. Maria Goossens, http://www.dokter-goossens.be/index.php?page=homeopathy.

Joette Calabrese, "All About Apis Mellifica-The Stinging Homeopathic Medicine," *Wellness Naturally* (blog), June 13, 2014, https://www.boironusa.com/blog/2014/archives/all-about-apis-mellifica-the-stinging-homeopathic-medicine/.

ACKNOWLEDGMENTS

With the writing of each book, I have the privilege of tapping into the expertise of many different people willing to help increase my knowledge and understanding of events and topics portrayed in the story.

I am sincerely grateful to Christophe Merville, the Director of Education and Pharmacy Development at Boiron USA. Christophe reviewed my chapters dealing with homeopathy and Marie's preparation of the *Apis mellifica* and how it would have been administered to the commandant. *Merci*, Christophe, for your input and support. I do hope we are able to meet face to face one day!

Our daughters, Laura Shonberg and Taya Gray, are always my first readers and provide a great first look at my early drafts. My dear friend Dominique Dailly continues to assist with all things French, helping ensure that my portrayal of my characters accurately reflects the French language and culture. Thank you, Orly Ziv-Maxim, for providing guidance and insight regarding the Holocaust.

With this third book, my talented sister, Kathleen Noble, has once again painted two original watercolors for the front and back covers. Thank you, Kathleen, for the beautiful works of original art, the covers of all of my books, that grace our home.

Sally Carr continues to be my editor extraordinaire. My three books in the Lavender Meuse Trilogy flow as they do across history and events because of your eagle eye and attention to detail. My characters love you, as do I.

To my husband Terry, thank you for loving my stories and being supportive and excited as the books go out into the world. You are truly my beloved.

Thank you most of all to my dedicated readers. I write for you.

READERS GUIDE

1. Marie was loved by both Henri and Tanvir. While she loved them both as well, her relationship with each man was very different. What does each love offer Marie, and what sacrifices does each require? Have you had a similar experience in your own life?

2. Throughout a story, characters often change. Which of the characters in *The Lavender Bees of Meuse* do you think changed the most and how? What was their motivation to change?

3. Have circumstances in your own life caused you to change in ways you could not have foreseen? How do you think these changes have affected your choices and decisions?

4. Is there one character in the books that you relate to the most? Why?

5. Bernard is a crusty character. He has been beside Marie throughout her journey in Meuse offering her support and protection, all the while maintaining his demeanor of reluctance and frustration. Who in your life has a similar personality and relationship with you?

6. Marie's life was shaped by how she lived it in response to two world wars. What events in your life do you feel have shaped you and the choices you have made in response to great challenges?

7. How has reading this book, or any of the Lavender Meuse Trilogy novels portraying the characters' lives from 1905–1946, impacted your understanding of this time in history?

CPSIA information can be obtained
at www.ICGtesting.com
Printed in the USA
FSHW021256300620
71699FS